MYSTERY ON CAPE COD

By

Adelaide Cummings

ISBN: 0-7596-8636-X

This book is printed on acid free paper.

1stBooks - rev. 05/03/02

CHAPTER ONE

Jeff Cahill woke with a start, routed from a deep sleep by the beat of rock and roll. Even his bed was vibrating. He tottered groggily to his feet, pulled on the clothes he'd laid out so carefully the night before, and ran across the hall to his sister's room.

"Peg!" he shouted above the din. "Get a move on and stop fooling around. Cut that thing off! Don't you remember? Mr. Hall's picking us up in an hour!"

A merry and excited face popped out like a jack-in-the-box. "Look who's talking! You're the one who nearly overslept!" Peg reached out, grabbed him by the sleeve and pulled him into her room.

"I've been ready for ages. Needed time to run through my favorites." She turned wistfully toward the CD player. "Do you think Cousin Lou might have one? At least a tape recorder?"

Jeff shook his head. "Not a chance. Bet there hasn't been anything new in her house for fifty years. What she'll have is an old crank-up gramophone with a horn, and some 1920 fox trots. What's the matter? Not getting cold feet, are you?"

"Of course not, silly. Anybody'd like to spend a vacation on Cape Cod. Just the same, I wouldn't want to go alone," Peg blurted.

1

"Me neither," Jeff admitted. "Well, you're not going to. Are you worried about Cousin Lou?" he asked, voicing his own anxiety.

"Guess so. I wish we knew what she's like. Do you remember her?"

"Not too well." Jeff wrinkled his forehead. "She only spent one night here about three years ago. Seems to me she wore flat brown shoes and a kind of hairy tweed skirt. Didn't say much, either."

"That's the way I remember her," said Peg unhappily.

"Oh well, she was smart enough to invite us." Jeff's voice was cheerful. "She can't be all that bad. Anyhow, we'll stick together." He spied his sister's suitcase, neatly tagged and tied with heavy cord. "Come on. I'll lug your stuff down now, and get mine after breakfast."

Out in the kitchen Mom was busy at the stove. Sunshine leaped across the window sill and spilled across the floor. Peg's spirits lifted. She grabbed Mom around the waist and gave her a big hug. "This is the day we've been waiting for! Think we might get there in time to go to the beach?"

Mom kept right on stirring the pot and didn't say a word. Jeff shot an inquiring glance at Peg.

"Sorry you aren't coming too, Mom," said Peg hastily. "But it's just for two weeks. Anyhow, you'll have fun helping Althea with your first grandchild." She turned to Jeff. "A nephew! Isn't that the greatest? What'll I make him call me? Aunt Peg, or Aunt Margaret?"

Mom turned around and put a steaming bowl of oatmeal in front of each of them. Now they could see her troubled face.

"Plenty of time to decide that later," she told them. "Right now you'd better put on your thinking caps and figure out how you're going to get to Cape Cod. I'm at my wit's end!"

Jeff froze to his spoon. "It was supposed to be all fixed up a week ago, right after the baby was born. You told us you couldn't take us, but that you'd found a ride for us..."

"And so I had," said Mom gently. "Let's just review it. Your Dad's off on his yearly two weeks of R.O.T.C. army duty. So I set up my own vacation from the plant for the same two weeks, and cleared it with Cousin Lou. This was a convenient time for her to have the three of us. Then Althea's baby came a month early, and she's due home from the hospital tomorrow. Cousin Lou agreed to have you two without me, and I heard that Mr. Hall from our church was vacationing on the Cape. He was glad for your company on the long drive..."

"So?" Jeff interrupted.

"So he telephoned an hour ago. He's been called to Philadelphia on business and has had to put off his visit to the Cape indefinitely. Oh dear!" she sighed. "I don't know where to turn. It all fit together so beautifully! Althea really needs me!"

"The ride's off?" asked Peg. "So we fly! Or would it cost too much?" she asked anxiously.

"I'm in a mood to forget the cost," said Mom, "but the airport's thirty miles from here. Anyhow, the plane would land you outside Boston. That's a long way from Cape Cod."

"What about a train?" urged Peg.

"There's no through train to the Cape," Mom explained. "There's a train to Boston, but none from there to the Cape. I can't very well ask Cousin Lou to drive eighty miles to meet you, now can I?"

"Guess that blows our trip then." Jeff's mouth was stiff with disappointment. "Wait a minute! What about a bus? Bound to be one of those. Couldn't we get to the Cape by bus?"

"Ye-es," nodded Mom. "There are connecting buses. Greyhound goes into Boston. The Bonanza line goes to Cape Cod from the same terminal. You'd have to change from one bus to the other, though, and get your luggage transferred. You two have never had that kind of responsibility. It's a lot to ask of ten year olds."

"It's a cinch," said Jeff firmly. "Peg and I aren't exactly helpless, Mom. Why don't you give us a chance?" He pointed to Peg's suitcase. "If you're going to stew about it, you could tag us! Like our suitcases," he urged. "Put us in the driver's charge. He'll turn us over to the next one..."

"In a hurry!" laughed Peg.

"If there's any kind of mixup, the man at the Boston ticket office can phone Cousin Lou. We've got sense enough to give him her number. Anyhow, he could read our tags."

"Now don't rush me. It's an idea, though." Mom was turning it over in her mind. "Let's take a look at the time-table, and see if there's a close connection. I wouldn't want you two stranded. You might land yourselves in all kinds of trouble!"

The time-table showed fifty minutes between the arrival of the Greyhound bus and the departure of the Bonanza.

"Nearly an hour!" pleaded Jeff. "That's plenty of time to make an old connection! From the same station, for Pete's sake!"

"Eat your breakfast and let me think about it," said Mom. "Where's Peg disappeared? Her breakfast will get cold."

"Right here!" Peg ran back into the kitchen carrying two luggage tags and Mom's magic marker pencil. "Just in case," she added anxiously.

"That might be called a handy hint," laughed Mom. "Well, I've decided. I'm going to let you do it. It certainly seems safe, and it fits the plans for each of us. Then too, I feel that Jeff made a point. It's time I let you stretch your wings. Cousin Lou's no spring chicken, and she's decidedly set in her ways. You'll be expected to adapt to them." She smiled. "Your dad says you couldn't change her mind with a bulldozer! I can't believe you'll have many

5

adventures, but at least you can be sure of some nice fresh air and some new experiences. Goodness, look at the time! Finish your breakfast, we've lots to do. The bus leaves in forty minutes."

Jeff bolted a last wedge of toast. "We can make it. I'll phone Cousin Lou and ask her to meet the afternoon bus from Boston. Peg, get moving on the box lunch. Lots of peanut butter and jelly sandwiches for me, and skip the lettuce."

Mom's eyes twinkled. "You're certainly taking charge, young man. I'm beginning to feel safe about putting Peg in your care. What job have you left for me?"

Jeff handed her the magic marker. "The most important one, Mom. The tags!"

CHAPTER TWO

Mom drove them to the bus terminal and spoke with the driver. He told her they'd surely make the connection to Boston. "With time to spare," he assured her. "Don't worry, Ma'am. Those two would be hard to lose!" He pointed to the tags, neatly pinned to Jeff's and Peg's blouses.

Please Deliver To

Miss Louise W. Bowman

Ellistown, Cape Cod, Massachusetts

Telephone: 528-5885

He led them down the aisle to the middle of the bus. "These are the most comfortable seats," he told them. "No fumes, and less swaying. Remember that, when you change to Bonanza."

Peg smiled at him and slipped into the window seat. She jiggled the lever. "Look, Jeff, see how the back lets down," she marveled. Then the two of them pressed their noses against the window and waved goodbye to Mom, who stayed right there waving back, until the bus pulled out.

Jeff watched until she became a tiny speck, then settled back with a happy sigh. "We made it! Things looked bad there for a while."

Peg kept on staring out the window and didn't answer. Jeff shot her a glance. What was the matter with her? Why did she look so scared? Then he remembered. She'd never spent a night away from home! He'd had two overnight hikes with the Cub Scouts, and the Scout Master had kept them busy every minute. Maybe that was the secret! He pulled two pencils and a little notepad from his pocket.

"Time for games," he said briskly. "You get first turn. What'll it be?"

"Tic-tac-toe!" Peg always chose that.

"Oh, alright," he grumbled. "But I've got a better one. We count animals and get points..."

"Wait for your turn!" Peg sat up straight and tapped briskly on his pad, her homesickness forgotten. "Right now it's tic-tac-toe!"

Two hours slipped quickly by. They played several games, then looked out the window at the lush New England countryside. They ate their sandwiches and dozed awhile. Soon they passed the big Connecticut tobacco farms and barns, then the bus pulled to a stop at New Haven. One of the passengers, an elderly lady, was getting off there. Jeff went inside the bus station and brought back two bottle of grape soda, not daring to be gone too long for fear the bus would leave without him.

He needn't have hurried. The bus driver was fussing with a large key which opened the luggage door outside the bus. He'd gotten it open easily enough, and had pulled out the old lady's luggage.

He'd stacked in the bags of the on-coming passengers. But when he slammed the door to close and lock it, it sprang back, then jammed. Now it was only partly closed.

"We stay right here until that door is closed and locked," the driver explained to a tall, tired looking grey-haired man who had just come aboard. "It might swing open on the highway and cause an accident. I'll have to call a serviceman. We'll need a hammer and crowbar to force it."

"What about our connection to Boston?" Jeff asked anxiously.

"I can't make any promises, sonny. We have nearly an hour's leeway, though." Other passengers crowded around him, asking questions and delaying him. Jeff could see that he was getting cross.

The tall passenger looked at Jeff and Peg.

"Cape Cod? That's where I'm headed. Don't worry, kids. My car's in Boston, and if we miss the connection you can come along with me."

Peg's face cleared, but Jeff was bothered. The last thing Mom had told him was not to talk to strangers. How could they possibly go off in a car with one?

It took forty-five minutes for the serviceman to get there, and it seemed even longer! Then they watched him do the repairs, but that took another twenty-five minutes.

"All aboard!" the driver called at last. "I'm going to try and catch up some lost time." He did very well, and he might have done even better if the traffic hadn't been as thick as porridge as they neared the city. Sitting nervously on the edge of their seats as the precious margin of time melted away, Jeff and Peg grew more and more frantic each time the bus came to a standstill behind the long line of backed up cars. They pulled into the bus terminal at Boston's Park Square exactly six minutes after the Cape Cod bus had left, and both of them were exhausted from the tension.

"The next bus to the cape is in about four hours, kids," the driver said kindly. "Step over there to the ticket agent behind the counter, and have him telephone the lady who's expecting you. Then wait here in the station. Sorry, but I've got to go right out again."

"Four hours!" groaned Peg. "That's as long as half a day of school!"

"It will seem longer that that with nothing to do," said the tall man. "Why don't you come along with me, kids? My car's in the parking lot across the street. I'm headed for Ellistown myself, and I know Miss Bowman."

What luck! Jeff opened his mouth to accept, but before he could get a word out, Peg put her mouth against his ear and whispered. He flushed. That was Peg for you! She'd spotted something that he'd missed.

"Sorry, sir," he said, grateful to his sister for letting him do the talking. He took a deep breath. "How do we know who you are, or where you're really from? You saw Cousin Lou's name, and Ellistown right on our tags! We'd better wait."

The man stared at him a second, then smiled. "Good for you, sonny. You're right to make sure." He pulled out his driver's license. "See? There's my name. Allan Clark. Sea View Lane, Ellistown, Massachusetts. Do I pass?"

"Sea View Lane? That's where Cousin Lou lives!" Peg's voice soared like a kite.

"So she does. We're neighbors. That is, our properties are side by side. I went to grade school with your Cousin Lou years and years ago. We were good friends."

Jeff stretched out his hand. "That's the best news ever, Mr. Clark. We're tickled! I'm Jeff Cahill, and this is my sister Peg."

"Thanks a million, Mr. Clark!" Then Peg turned to her brother. "Quick, Jeff. Give me some change so I can get the ticket man to phone Cousin Lou, the way we promised if there was any change of plans."

But Mr. Clark was rounding up their bags. "Let's go, kids. If we leave right away we can beat the bus to Ellisville. Is this all your luggage? Don't leave anything behind!"

"Jeff!" said Peg stubbornly. "We've got to make that phone call. We learned that at home, at school,

11

everyplace. It won't take two minutes of Mr. Clark's time." Off she ran.

In no time she came running back. "It's O.K.," she panted. "But Jeff, do you think Cousin Lou is deaf?"

"Nope. At least I don't remember her that way. Why?"

"Because when the station man asked her, 'Do you know a Mr. Clark?' she yelled so loud that I could hear her as well as he could. You know how deaf folks yell on the phone. Then we got cut off and I didn't have any more money to call back. But it's all right!"

"You haven't told us what she yelled," Jeff reminded her.

"She hollered, 'Know him? I should say I do. For about forty years!'" She looked anxiously at Mr. Clark. "You do understand? We've been trained to double check. Even if we believe what we're told..."

"Of course I understand. Now let's get out of here in a hurry."

They piled into Mr. Clark's car. He paid the parking attendant and they were on their way, headed for the Southeast Expressway to Cape Cod.

"This sure beats the bus station waiting room!" Jeff let out a grateful breath. "Do you work in Ellistown, Mr. Clark? I thought it was just a village."

Mr. Clark adjusted his rear view mirror. "So it is, and a small one at that. But it's only a few miles from

Woods Hole.   Maybe you've heard of the famous Oceanographic Institute there."

"You bet!"   Jeff sat bolt upright.   "Are you an oceanographer, sir? I've never met one."

Mr. Clark couldn't help smiling.   "Well, you're seeing one in the flesh son. But we're not such a strange breed of cats. You'll find we're no different from   most   scientists.   In   fact,   that's   what oceanography is, a combination of many sciences..."

"What kind of things do oceanographers do?" Peg asked timidly.   "Jeff knows more about them than I do."

"That's a big question, young lady. But I'll give you a few examples. How big would you say a test tube is?"

"About as long as your hand and as thick as your middle finger," Peg shot back promptly.

"Right you are. Well, give me <u>one</u> test tube filled with ocean water and turn me loose in my lab. I'll be able to tell you <u>what</u> <u>ocean</u> <u>that</u> <u>seawater</u> <u>came</u> <u>from</u>. Indian Ocean, Caribbean, Atlantic, Pacific, you name it."

"You can?" Jeff was goggle eyed. "I thought all seawater was alike!"

"Well it isn't. It varies in all kinds of ways. It's saltier in hot climates where there's more evaporation. Near shore there are the minerals that have washed into it from the land, and those vary from place to

13

place. Way out in the great depths there are other particles carried by the currents…"

"That makes you a kind of detective with lots of clues to follow!" exclaimed Peg.

"Exactly. That's where the fun comes in." He glanced at Jeff. "Tell me, have you ever taken a plug out of a watermelon, or cored an apple?"

"Lots of times. So has Peg." Jeff couldn't imagine what was coming next.

"Then you'll understand what I mean when I tell you that we spend a lot of time coring the ocean floor. Same kind of procedure. We push down heavy tubes with sharp cutting edges and pull up plugs from the sea floor. Layers and layers of compacted ooze that have drifted down over the centuries. That ooze has been accumulating undisturbed for hundreds of thousand of years. Mind you, there's no wind down there to disturb it. The layers are like the rings of a tree, and we can tell their age. Sometimes we uncover some sort of extinct fossilized creature trapped in a particular layer and we are able to determine its period in time."

"Wow! That what I'd like to be, an oceanographer!" declared Jeff.

"My own boy says the same thing, and he reads everything he can lay his hands on. Asks questions, too, by the dozen. He's about your age. Wish I thought he'd have behaved as sensibly as you did, back at the bus station. I should have identified myself right off."

Jeff turned pink. He didn't know what to answer, so he changed the subject. "What's your boy's name, sir?"

"Eric. He's nine, but he seems more like eleven or twelve to me. That's because he's had so much responsibility dumped on him this past year. Hard to realize he's only in the fourth grade when I expect him to act like a grown man."

"Jeff and I are in fifth," volunteered Peg. "Maybe he can come over and hang out with us tomorrow."

Mr. Clark seemed to hesitate. "We'll see. Perhaps you'd better clear it with your Cousin Lou." He peered ahead of him. "Why, there's the bus!" He appeared relieved. "We've caught up with it. I'll pull ahead and flag it down."

"What for?" asked Peg. "We didn't leave anything."

"To put you aboard. Your Cousin Lou will be meeting that bus. It might be simpler if she found you on it, according to plan. Less explanations." He stepped on the accelerator, shot a hundred yards ahead, then stopped his car and stepped out, waving his arms. The bus halted. Mr. Clark tossed out two suitcases from the back seat and spoke to the driver.

"Here are two left-behinds, from the delayed Greyhound bus. Drop them off at Ellistown," he said.

The driver nodded. "Miss Bowman told me about them, and asked me to keep an eye on them. I was wondering where they were." He stowed the luggage, jumped back in, waved and pulled away.

15

Jeff and Peg found two seats in the middle section of the bus.

"Whew!" Peg wiped her forehead. "We've been climbing on and off these old things all day. Glad this is the last one."

Jeff didn't answer.

"What's the matter, Jeff? Are you mad or something?" Peg peered at him anxiously.

"Of course not, silly. I was only wondering...What do you think about Mr. Clark and the way he acted just now?"

"How do you mean? I thought he was nice..."

"Oh sure, at first! I thought so too. He was great about telling us things and answering questions. I was really looking forward to the rest of the drive. Then you asked his boy to come over and it was like a curtain falling. He couldn't get rid of us fast enough. Why else do you suppose he dumped us on this bus instead of driving us all the way?"

"He told us..."

"Oh Peg, honestly!" Jeff was out of patience. "You can't believe everything people tell you! What he told us didn't make sense! He'll beat this crate to Ellistown easy as pie. He's already miles ahead of us and he lives practically next door to Cousin Lou! He could have taken us right to her house. Before she every left to meet the bus!"

Peg nodded slowly. "He didn't want me to phone her, either, come to think of it. He knew it wouldn't take me a minute!"

"There's more. It didn't hit me then, but it does now. He was talking about going to school with Cousin Lou and he made a slip. He said 'We were friends'…Wouldn't you expect him to say 'We <u>are</u> friends'? If they still are, that is. I think the whole thing's cockeyed, don't you?"

"I think it's fun!" Peg bounced happily on her seat. "It's like something on T.V. '<u>The</u> <u>Case</u> <u>of</u> <u>the</u> <u>Strange</u> <u>Oceanographer</u>'. Oh, Jeff, this day is really picking up! We haven't even gotten to Ellistown, and already there's a mystery!"

CHAPTER THREE

Cousin Lou was waiting for them at the little Ellistown crossroad where the bus stopped. Jeff, leaning against the window as the bus pulled in, spied her cheerful, sun-browned face and her starched cotton dress. His spirits lifted. She looked a lot nicer than he remembered!

She enfolded them both in a welcoming bear-hug, but she didn't say much. He's been right about that much, Cousin Lou had a way of coming right to the point.

"Good trip, I hope. Glad you got here all of a piece."

"Oh, Cousin Lou, we almost didn't get here at all!" The whole story came tumbling out of Peg. She didn't leave out a thing...the big disappointment at breakfast, Jeff's idea about the tags...She described the jammed bus door, the delay in New Haven, the missed connection in Boston. "We'd still be stuck there, except for the nice man," she ended. "He popped us in his car and caught up with the Cape Cod bus."

"What man?" Cousin Lou's eyebrows shot up. "Land sakes, don't you two know enough not to take up with strangers?"

"We know that much, Cousin Lou!" Jeff's tone was frosty. "He wasn't exactly a stranger. Not to you, anyhow. He showed us his driver's license and everything. Mr. Allan Clark from right here in Ellistown, and he lives next door to you!"

"Oh." Cousin Lou paused. "So that's what that phone call was about—Got cut off." She frowned, then shrugged. "Well, you're here safe and sound. That's what counts."

Peg dug her elbows into Jeff's ribs. "We liked him ever so much, Cousin Lou. Do you?"

"I don't hold with discussin' my neighbors." Cousin Lou clipped out. "Now, pile into my old Jeep and let's get home to supper."

Peg and Jeff did as they were told. Cousin Lou grabbed hold of the steering wheel like a drowning swimmer clutching a life preserver. She stepped on the throttle and the old car went into a fit of hiccups. It gave a few wheezes and shakes, then moved ahead. Peg would have laughed if she hadn't been afraid to.

They turned off the main road, into a hard-packed dirt lane skirted by a ragged stone wall. On the right was pasture land, filigreed with daisies and Queen Anne's Lace. On the left, across meadows and marshes, they could make out rolling sand dunes, and hear the swooshing sound of ocean waves breaking on the beach. The air had a spanking clean, salty tang, and smelled of hay drying in the sun. They rounded a bend, and there by the side of the road was a little box of a Cape Cod house topped by a massive brick center-chimney rampant with ivy. The roof and sides of the house were shingled and weather-worn. Hollyhocks peered over a picket fence, standing at attention like sentinels.

"Oh!" gasped Peg. "Cousin Lou's house looks like a candy box!"

"It looks the way it's looked for the past hundred and fifty years," snorted Cousin Lou, but there was pride in her voice.

Inside, it was spic and span and smelled of beeswax. The wide floorboards were hand-pegged, and covered with fading braided rugs. In an old pine rocking chair, a butterscotch cat was curled up, front paws over its nose, snoozing. It wasn't easy to tell where the cat ended and the chair began. The biggest fireplace they had ever seen extended along one entire wall, and right in the middle was a crane, hung with a big iron pot. Old pewter plated lined the mantle, set with a blue jug of daisies and Black-Eyed Susans. It was a homey house, filled with delicious smells. Peg sniffed hungrily.

"We eat supper in the kitchen," Cousin Lou told them. "Save the looking 'round until tomorrow. Mind you, I don't believe in idle hands. You'll be expected to set right to it, and do your chores first thing. When they're properly done, then your time's your own. Tonight I won't even let you help with the dishes. You've come a far piece and must be tuckered."

They ate stew and johnny cake, and little new garden peas. "Where do we sleep?" asked Peg, dousing cream on her raspberries. Her head was nodding.

"I've put you downstairs, child, in the room next to mine. It's 'bout as big as a pocket handkerchief, but it will be all yours. Jeff, you're upstairs under the eaves."

Jeff brought in Peg's suitcase, then lugged his own upstairs. He remembered carrying the same luggage that very morning. So much had happened that a week seemed to stretch in between.

He undressed quickly, reviewing the whole day in his mind, and the strange and brief encounter with Mr. Clark. The man had seemed so likeable, with his thick grey hair all crinkly like new steel wool, and his tired, kind eyes. It was hard to figure out why he'd gone out of his way to befriend them, and then had gotten rid of them so hastily. It didn't make sense!

Jeff threw himself across his bed next to the window and looked out. It was still early, and the long June twilight cast shadows across the lawn. Here and there a firefly dipped and flickered. He drew a deep breath. His sheets were so deliciously cool and smelled of sunlight and fragrant pine. Behind the sand dunes he heard the breakers relentlessly pounding the beach. A whiff of lilacs drifted up and mingled with other unknown fragrances from Cousin Lou's cool and scented garden. He closed his eyes and fell into a deep sleep.

It must have been several hours later when something woke him. He sat bolt upright and looked out. It was pitch dark in his room. Outside the sky was lightly dusted with stars, and a young moon shone brightly. The big elm near his window cast an

21

ebony shadow on the ground below. From the highest reaches of the tree poured a gabble of chittering noise. Back and forth it went...like a pair of quarrelsome old ladies having an argument. The noises would stop and start, stop and start, growing louder and faster.

What could it be? Jeff knelt on his bed, opened the window screen and stuck his head out. He looked straight up, for the great tree towered overhead, high above the rooftop. The leaves, large and thickly packed together, screened the branches. He couldn't make out a thing. A gust of wind stirred the ancient elm, and all those blurred and swaying leaves made him dizzy. Then a ragged wisp of clouds scudded across the moon, and darkness dropped like a hood across the lawn. The weird chitter of the unknown creatures stopped at once.

There was no possible way to tell what was up there, making those spine-tingling noises! Suddenly Jeff jerked his head back in. Suppose there were wildcats out there, or panthers, who might spring down on him!

He slammed down the screen and jumped back into bed, drawing the sheet up close under his chin. Except for the waves it now seemed totally quiet, but as he listened, the undertone of night sounds seemed to grow louder and louder, fracturing the stillness...the rusty monotonous rasp of the croakers in the marshes, the high insistent trill of the crickets. An owl hooted, off in the dark perimeter of the woods, and its weird and lonely call seemed to hang on the air. Jeff scrunched further down, thinking longingly of his familiar bed at home. Now he knew for sure that he'd be awake all night! But once again the music of the sea-sounds worked its magic, and sleep overtook him.

At breakfast, Cousin Lou got a big laugh. "We don't have panthers and wildcats here in the Cape," she told him. You heard Rascal and Bandit. They're a real nuisance, those two! When the moon's out, such a fuss they make!"

"Rascal and Bandit?" asked Peg. "Are they your cats?"

Cousin Lou shook her head. "Just names that seemed right for wild creatures. A pair of raccoons. Ever seen any?"

"Not for real. Only in picture books."

"Cute little fellows." Cousin Lou's weathered face broke into a smile. "Beady eyes with white rings around them. Little pointed black faces. And such clever fingers. Found that out in jig time!"

"What happened?" asked Jeff.

"Eggs began to run short. One dark night I set out to catch the thief."

"How'd you plan to do that?" Jeff looked at her with awe. Imagine, tiny Cousin Lou tackling a thief!

"I was going to bash him a good one with my big black spider."

"Your <u>what</u>?" Peg was round-eyed.

23

Cousin Lou laughed. "That's a country word you city folks don't use. It stands for big iron frying pan. Anyhow, I hid behind a lilac bush, heard a rustle and flashed a light. Those two coons flipped open the hook-and-eye fastening of the henhouse door 'bout as well as you could."

"Wish I'd seen it," said Peg. "So then what did you do?"

"Banged on my pan to scare them away. Next morning I put on a better lock."

"Do you think we'll see them? Hope so," said Jeff.

"Not likely. You'll hear them, though. All week, while the moon's out."

"Couldn't care less, now that I know that's causing it. Raccoons! What do you know? I didn't have a clue!" marveled Jeff.

"How about our chores?" Peg broke in impatiently. "Let's do them, and then go exploring."

"Fair enough." Cousin Lou handed her a small willow basket. "Your job's to feed the chickens and gather up the eggs."

Peg took the basket eagerly. "What do they eat and where are the eggs, Cousin Lou?"

"One question at a time, child. You'll feed them laying mash, and give them fresh water. I'll show you, this once, and help you collect the eggs. Tomorrow I'll expect you to do the job yourself."

"How about me?" asked Jeff anxiously.

"What willing workers!" smiled Cousin Lou. "Hope it doesn't wear off. Jeff, you're to go to the stable and turn old Nelly out to pasture. She's a gentle old roan mare. You two will enjoy riding her. Wash down her stall, then bring in fresh hay to make her a clean bed. Can you manage that?"

"Never have, but just watch me!" Jeff was already at the door. He paused. "She won't kick me, will she?"

"Not Nelly. Don't startle her. Speak to her, and stroke her nose. Take her a lump of sugar, if you like. Then open her stall and let her out. Now come along, Peg."

In less than an hour, both Jeff and Peg had done their tasks. "What's all the flap about chores?" asked Jeff. "We didn't mind them a bit. They were fun!"

"Might change your mind before your visit's up," said Cousin Lou dryly. "Now where are you two going to explore?"

Jeff and Peg looked at each other. He spoke for both of them. "We just want to fool around. Maybe we'll walk over and look at the ocean."

"This afternoon I'm taking you to the town beach. It has a lifeguard on duty. Wait until then. You wouldn't be safe, alone in these breakers."

"Oh, we wouldn't go in," Peg promised. "We just want to walk the dunes and see the big waves. We've never seen the ocean."

"Go ahead, then. I'll trust you to abide by your word. Walk straight down Sea View Lane and turn off on the first path to your left. It takes you around Salt Pond. The dunes are behind that. Mind you, get yourselves back at lunchtime. I like my meals to run off on time. Laggards lose out!"

"How are we 'sposed to know when?" asked Peg.

"Go by your stomachs. They're apt to be reliable. Now shoo! I've got a blueberry pie to make."

"Oh boy! We don't want to miss out on that! Come on, Peg. I'm starting to get hungry right now." Jeff grabbed his sister's hand. "Who needs clocks? They're for city folks!"

Cousin Lou couldn't help smiling as she turned back to the house. Jeff and Peg had been here less than twenty-four hours, and already they were talking like Cape Codders!

CHAPTER FOUR

Peg and Jeff followed Cousin Lou's simple directions, heading down a lane bordered with honeysuckle and wild rugosa roses. Behind the ditches filled with purple beach-peas and delicate cinnamon fern, scrub oak sprouted in the sandy soil and crouched low against the wind. They could hear the sweet, clear notes of a meadowlark over in the cedar ridge, and the sharp and unfamiliar peewee calls of the piping plover. The Cape's usual early morning fog was lifting rapidly, and only an occasional wisp remained in the pockets of the hollows. They admired the soft green of the bayberry clumps and the moon-pale blossoms of the beachplum bushes. They turned left and began circling the salt pond that lay between them and the dunes. Lime-green marsh grass shimmered at its edges where fat cattails thrust up to astonishing heights. Out in the middle, on a protruding rock, an unblinking old Goliath heron hunched like a venerable Judge, refusing to be routed by intruders. Then Jeff saw something he'd almost overlooked. He tugged at Peg's sleeve.

"Look!" he pointed. "What's that guy doing? Craziest fishing I ever saw!"

A deeply tanned boy with corntassel hair was standing in the pond only about ten feet from the bank. In front of him was a floating slat basket set into an automobile's inner tube. They could see the pole of a long, strange tool in his hand. He seemed to be busily scratching and digging at something on the bottom of the pond.

"What are you looking for?" called Jeff.

"Quahogs." The boy kept right on digging.

"Must be some kind of foreigner," said Peg. "He doesn't talk English."

The boy stared at them. "Quahogs. They're a special kind of clam Cape Cod's famous for. You two must be strangers."

Strangers! A bell rang in Jeff's mind. "Say, is your name Eric Clark?"

"How did you know?" Eric straightened up and stopped digging. He ran a cautious eye over them. "Have I ever seen you? Don't think so!"

Jeff shook his head. "Your Dad told us about you when he drove us part way down here, yesterday afternoon. We're Jeff and Peg Cahill. We asked him to let you come over today. To Cousin Lou Bowman's. That's where we're staying."

"Didn't he tell you?" asked Peg, giving Jeff a poke.

"Nope." Eric shook his head. "Funny he didn't mention it. I hope you're going to stick around awhile," he added anxiously. "It's kind of lonely, way off here at the end of the lane, now that school's out. I know lots of things to do."

"Will you show us how to dig quahogs?" Jeff and Peg were hopping around like a string of firecrackers ready to go off.

"Whoa there! They're not going to run away!" laughed Eric. "It's easy. See those little round places over there in the shallows?"

"Like upside-down air bubbles?" Peg bent over and peered.

"Seems to me they look more like those moon craters on T.V. Anyhow, watch." Eric thrust the pronged end of his pole down and gently pulled it up, wet blobs of sand clinging to it. He popped the blob into his floating bucket. "Boy, are these ever good! Say, we ought to have a clambake on the beach some night soon."

"How would we cook them?" asked Peg.

"In a barrel. First you dig a pit, and line it with rocks. Then you add charcoal and get a hot fire going. You layer the barrel…"

"Do <u>what</u>? More foreign lingo!" laughed Jeff.

"Fill it up in layers. A layer of seaweed, a layer of clams, more seaweed, then lobsters, sweet corn and potatoes, and so on. Add sea water, and boil away! Everything has the best flavor ever! You top off the whole blast with watermelon!"

"Sounds great. Hope we do have a clambake." Jeff and Peg had already rolled up their dungarees and they were bending over, using their hands like forked prongs. Eric's floating bucket began to fill up.

"Got more than we'll need at home," he said. "Want to take some back to Miss Bowman? She might make you a chowder for tonight. You're going to like quahog chowder!"

"Fine." Jeff leaned over and tested the bucket's weight. "This load's, heavy, though. Let's leave it here awhile, and pick it up later. Come on, let's climb to the top of the dunes. Peg and I want to see the ocean. We've been hearing it ever since we got here."

"Good idea. That'll give my dungarees time to dry off," said Eric. "I wouldn't want to drip all over Miss Bowman's kitchen. She'd shoo me off in a hurry! And give me the back of her tongue to boot!"

"Maybe," said Peg. "And maybe not. Jeff and I haven't had time to decide about Cousin Lou. We keep changing our minds."

The dunes were surprisingly high. Great shafts of silvery seagrass sprouted on them, bending and waving gracefully in the wind. Each wave deposited a glistening, scalloped border on the sand, which was quickly absorbed as the wave retreated. It was as regular as the metronome on Peg's piano at home. Further down the beach, small sandpipers were daintily pecking for food in the gleaming reaches of the surf. Sunlight caught the spray and sent out rainbows of color. Overhead, herring gulls, dipping and wheeling like stunt pilots, made little mewling cries. Most of them were banking and sailing, riding the updraft of the wind, but occasionally one would swoop down behind the dunes, into the salt pond, and rise out of its dive with a clam in its hooked beak. Then the gull would fly down the beach where there was a flat-topped sea wall. Hovering like a glider, it would drop the clam directly on the hard stone surface, then swoop down and land on it.

"What are those gulls doing?" Peg pointed in their direction.

"Cracking open clamshells by dropping them on the wall. Then they eat the clams," explained Eric.

"Pretty smart! I'll never call Peg a bird-brain again," said Jeff. "What would the gulls use, without the sea-wall?"

"Big rocks and boulders. Plenty of those along New England beaches!"

"You know a lot, don't you?" Jeff looked admiringly at the younger boy. "Peg and I come from the middle of Pennsylvania. This is brand new to us."

Eric shrugged. "I've always lived around here. You can't help noticing the tide and the sea, and sea creatures. Gets to be a part of you. I was lucky about Old Joe, too. He taught me ever so much. He knows more about things that live outdoors than anybody."

"Who's he?" asked Peg. "Your big brother?"

Eric laughed. "No, not exactly. He's about eighty. Been here most as long as anybody can remember. Look over there." He pointed down the beach, behind the dunes. Jeff and Peg had to look carefully to make out a weathered, tumble-down shack that seemed to melt into the background.

"One big wind would blow that old wreck to kingdom-come!" exclaimed Jeff.

31

"Even a big sneeze might do it," added Peg.

"Don't I know it! I do plenty of worrying about it. Dad says Old Joe used to be the best fishing guide in these parts. Can't remember that far back, but even a couple of years ago he kept his place ship-shape. I spent most of my spare time with him, and he sure taught me a lot! It's not the same without him." Eric's voice caught.

"Oh. But if he's dead, no wonder the shack's run down. What would you expect?" asked Peg.

"He's not dead, he still lives there. He's turned queer this past year, though. Runs from folks, even from me. Haven't laid eyes on him in ages, or spent a Saturday with him. He doesn't take any better care of himself than his shack, either. Guess he's too old."

"Does he get enough to eat?" asked Jeff.

"I'm sure about that, anyway. My Aunt Kate lives with us, and she sends me over once a week with staples and canned goods. I set them outside the shack, regular as clockwork. A few years back, though, Old Joe could live like a king. And not only off the sea. Off the land."

"Live off the land?" Peg's eyes popped. "you mean like BEARS?"

Eric couldn't help laughing. "More like Indians. Or Pilgrims. He showed me where to find sorrel and yarrow and tansy and fennel, and how to use young fiddlegreens. Medicinal plants too, like horehound and spearmint and colicroot, and some great stuff called jewelweed that takes the itch out of poison ivy.

Lots of time I get up at daybreak and garner a batch to sell."

"Did you say to <u>sell</u>?" asked Jeff. "Who'd buy that stuff?"

"Health Food stores. That's a big thing today. You're welcome to help me some morning and I'll share with you. But you'll have to shake yourself out of the sack before sun-up!"

"Great! I'd sure like to, if you'll teach me." Jeff's eyes were gleaming. "I'm beginning to see what you mean about Old Joe and why you worry about him. But what's the matter with the rest of the folks in Ellistown? If he comes from here and can't look after himself, why don't they help him, for Pete's sake?"

"You don't know Cape Codders," said Eric. "Folks 'round here believe in minding their own business. Dad went to see him awhile back, and I know for sure that he tried to help. Nothing came of it, though. I tried to talk to Dad about it but he wouldn't say much. They had some kind of quarrel. But why would Dad quarrel with that old guy? It beats me!"

"Let's go take a peek in the window," suggested Peg. "Maybe we can find a clue, or something."

"Do you really want to?" asked Eric doubtfully.

"Sure," said Jeff. "Why not? He'll be off someplace. Who'd hang around a dark old shack on a day like this?"

The three of them crept down the beach. All of them began to feel a little nervous, but no one wanted to admit it.

"This was your idea, Peg," said Jeff, when they reached the shack. "We'll let you do the peeking. You can tell us what you see."

"Thanks," said Peg weakly. Then her voice brightened. "I'm not tall enough. You do it!"

But Jeff and Eric had caught each others' wrists and interwoven them basket fashion. "Up you go," said Eric. They gave her a boost. She braced her elbows against the sill, then pressed her nose against the grimy, uncurtained window.

"It's pitch dark inside," she reported. "Can't see a thing."

At that moment the shack door banged and the startled boys dropped her with a thud. They all turned around, and stood frozen to the spot.

A ragged bundle of fury confronted them. From beneath long, matted hair, the old man's eyes glowered with rage. The three of them could feel his anger, like radiant heat. For a moment his loose mouth worked soundlessly. The he began to yell and flay his arms.

"Git off my place, varmints! Git off! It's mine, and nobody ain't gonna put me off! You!" He pointed a long dirty finger at Eric. "Spyin' on me! Git off and stay off, and that goes for your pappy too! Like as not he put you up to it. Git!" He waved his arms wildly.

They needed no urging. The three of them turned and ran. They kept right on running until they shot right over the sand dunes. Then, safely out of sight, they fell gasping on the grassy shore of the salt pond.

"So that's your nice old pal!" panted Jeff. "Well, you can have him!"

"My share too," said Peg. She shuddered. "He looked like the Wild Man in the freak show."

Eric frowned. "So what? Isn't that exactly what I tried to tell you?" He shook his head stubbornly. "Right up till last year he was the best friend I ever had, and I'm not apt to forget it. I'm not apt to forget the things he taught me, either. Like fishing and trapping, and how to gage the weather and salt-water farming…"

"What kind of farming?" Jeff couldn't believe his ears.

"Tell you what. I'll show you, it's too hard to explain. Tomorrow morning. How about meeting me here at the pond at nine o'clock?"

"Not a chance," moaned Peg. "Jeff and I will be slaving away by then. We have mountains of chores to do. Every single day!"

"That's right, those old chores! They'd slipped my mind." Jeff stopped, and began to laugh. "Cousin Lou sure hit the target on that! Guess we don't much sound like 'willing workers' any more!"

"Then let's make it ten o'clock. I'm busy as a pup with three cats to chase, myself," said Eric. "A screen to mend at home, then two lawns to mow, and bait to get down to the marina by daybreak. Ten o'clok suits me better. Wear your bathing suits and sneakers, though. That's important."

"Bathing suits! Say, I've just remembered. We're supposed to go off to a special beach this afternoon. One with a lifeguard. Want to come, Eric? Cousin Lou won't care," said Jeff.

"You bet," said Eric. "I know the beach you mean and it's a good one. Been too busy to get there this year. What time?"

"Cousin Lou didn't say. Let's take the clams home and ask her. Besides, I'm hungry."

The two boys each grabbed hold of the bucket handle and the three of them started briskly back toward Cousin Lou's.

"My, that long grass is pretty," said Peg as they skirted the Salt Pond. "Has it got a name?"

"Eel grass. See how it sort of floats on top of the water?"

"Can't we stop and pick some? I'd like to try and weave a basket for Mom."

Eric shook his head. "Forget it. Old Joe would skin you alive if he caught you. He says summer folks are nature's worst enemies. Oh, I'm sure you didn't know any better," he added hastily.

"Still don't," said Peg stubbornly. "What's the harm in taking a few old shafts? Who'd miss them?"

"The sea creatures, that's who," explained Eric. "Those shafts are shelter for crabs and blowfish and minnows. Scallop seeds, too. They helped us make our big haul this morning."

"Oh." Peg's voice was small.

"Take the Salt Pond," continued Eric. "Know how long it took to form? Over <u>twenty thousand years</u>!"

"Says who?" Jeff hooted. "Old Joe? How would he know?"

"My Dad says so, and he ought to know. He's studied marine biology. He throws a fit when speculators buy up the marshlands and fill them in for house lots and shopping centers. You should see the birds that come in here to nest. Herons and terns and grebes and yellowlegs and ospreys. Curlews too, and cormorants, and lots more."

"I'd sure like to," said Jeff. "But I wouldn't know what I was looking at. I've never seen most of the ones you named."

"Cousin Lou's got a bird book," Peg told him. "I saw it on the shelf next to the living room window. We could study it!"

They walked along a bit. "Whew, this bucket's getting heavy," complained Jeff. "Let's set it down a minute."

The boys blew on their hands and picked up the bucket again. "We did make a good haul," said Jeff as they trudged into the kitchen a few minutes later. "Cousin Lou, maybe you already know our friend Eric

37

Clark." Too late he remembered that they hadn't wiped their feet.

Cousin Lou noticed it too, but she didn't comment. Instead she put her hands on her hips and gave Eric a good long, searching stare. "Known Eric since he was a little mewling baby," she said. "Haven't laid eyes on him in a year or more."

"He's brought you some quahogs." Peg rolled out the strange new word, proud of herself for remembering.

"Quahogs? Been wanting some. They're scarcer'n hens teeth this year. Now that's right neighborly of you, Eric. These would fetch a good price at the fish pier. My! You do favor your father!"

"Folks say so." Eric shuffled his feet. "Well, guess I'll shove off home to lunch."

"Cousin Lou, couldn't Eric go with us this afternoon?" asked Jeff.

Cousin Lou considered a moment. "Can't seem to think of a single reason why not," she said at last.

"Let's make a early start," urged Peg. "What time will we pick him up?"

"Oh." Cousin Lou frowned and bit her lip. Then her face cleared. "Might as well stay right here for lunch, Eric, and save trouble all around. Go phone your Aunt Kate. If she's home, that is."

"Yes ma'am. Today's Saturday, and the library closes at noon. Thanks." Eric went down the hall to telephone.

"I'll set out the lunch," said Cousin Lou briskly. "Jeff, you can carry the plates to the table, time I've dished up. Peg, set another place, and pour that boy a big glass of milk. He looks as scrawny as a spring eel."

"How 'bout me? What can I do?" asked Eric, from the doorway.

"Fetch the blueberry pie," Cousin Lou told him. "I set it to cool in the pantry window."

The pie was so good they ate every bit of it.

"Wow! I'm torpedoed!" Jeff pushed back his chair with a happy sigh.

"Best way I know to fill up the holes," added Eric.

"You'll sink like stones after all that," said Cousin Lou. But she seemed pleased. "Never did like to see folks peck at their food. Remember though, one whole hour of making sand forts on the beach before you set foot in the water. Come along now, and I'll drop you off. Got about two hours' shopping to do."

They climbed into the jeep and Cousin Lou started down Sea View Lane. Then Eric clapped his forehead.

"Gosh, Miss Bowman, I'll have to go home after all. For my bathing suit."

"That's so. Wouldn't you know it!" Cousin Lou shrugged her shoulders and swung the jeep around, frowning. "Well, can't be helped."

In a minute she drew up before gate-posts that bordered a long graveled drive. Jeff and Peg could see a low, rambling stone house set far back at the end.

"Out with you, boy. Run fetch your suit, and bring a towel." Cousin Lou switched off the ignition. It was clear that she didn't intend to turn into the Clark driveway. Eric, looking a little surprised, did as he was told. Peg opened her mouth, but Jeff gave her a sharp nudge and she closed it quickly.

At last they were underway. The weather was perfect for an afternoon at the beach.

"Jeff and Peg," Cousin Lou told them, "I'm taking you to the edge of the new National Seashores Park. It came about while John Kennedy was President. How he loved Cape Cod!"

"We've read about his house at Hyannis Port," said Jeff. "Could you drive us up to see it someday?"

"Certainly not!" Cousin Lou was emphatic. "Those folks like their privacy, same's anybody. They don't want a lot of nosy trippers and summer people gawking at them!"

Eric cocked an eyebrow at Jeff, and saw that he was feeling snubbed.

"Peg and Jeff ought to see the great dunes," he added hastily. "They're a sight to see!"

"Too far for now," said Cousin Lou. "Some other day, if we make an early start.

"What's so special about the great dunes?" asked Peg.

"Well, take the ones at Truro. On a windy day you can spread your jacket, jump right off, and get blown back!"

"Expect us to swallow that?" Jeff scoffed.

"Ask Miss Bowman!" Eric turned to her for confirmation.

"Can't say as I ever tried it myself," said Cousin Lou. "But I mind the time your Dad did it, years ago. He was the most daring boy in the whole school." She smiled, remembering a gusty September day and a class picnic long ago.

"He was? Am I ever glad to hear it! Wait till I remind him, next time he jumps on me for being foolhardy!"

"You'll do nothing of the sort!" barked Cousin Lou. "He'd be bound to know you heard it from me. I'll thank you not to mention my name to your father!" She quivered like the lid of a pot coming to a boil.

The three of them shrank back against the cracked leather seat. Cousin Lou stabbed the accelerator like a jockey applying the spur, and the old car leaped ahead, groaning and shivering in protest. Now they were devouring the miles in great gulps, and all the while the silence was drawn so tight it seemed to creak.

"Here we are," said Cousin Lou after what seemed forever. "Now jump out, and make sure you keep out of mischief for the next two hours."

They shot from the car like bullets from a gun. "See what Peg means about Cousin Lou?" grumbled Jeff. "One minute she's sweet as pie, next minute she snaps your head off. I can't figure out why. She just blows her stack for no reason."

"Seems to me it mostly has something to do with your father," said Peg. "What did he ever do to her?"

"No clue." Eric shrugged. "I did ask Dad why she'd stopped coming 'round. She used to be right neighborly. You know, bringing jelly and stuff..."

"What did he say?" inquired Peg.

A grin wreathed Eric's face. "He said she'd better watch out, or she'd turn into a sour old maid." He looked embarrassed. "I'm not much good at figuring out grown-ups. Let's go swimming!"

Afterwards, when the whole beautiful day was ruined for him, Jeff thought back on the golden afternoon that the three of them had enjoyed together. The sun reflecting off the water in a million sparkling pinpoints of light—the white sand, all soft and sunwarmed, the continuous rows of white-crested breakers marching like soldiers in endless ranks, then toppling over in eddying swirls of froth and foam as they hit the beach...Peg ventured out waist-deep and even swam a few strokes.

"Watch! The salt water's holding me up!" she marveled. "Couldn't sink if I tried!"

"Well, don't try too hard," laughed Eric. "We'll fix it so you can swim like a seal, even in an old fresh-water swimming pool back home."

42

"Wish we could stay forever," sighed Peg.

Jeff felt the same way. How could he possibly know that all the day's joy would drain away before nightfall?

Cousin Lou picked them up on schedule, and she seemed in a better mood. "Guess I was kind of testy, earlier," she admitted. "Bought some salt water taffy to sweeten my disposition." She passed the bag around. But again, when they reached Eric's house, she dropped him off at the front of his long driveway instead of turning into his door.

By the time Peg and Jeff reached home, they were hungry again. "Shake the sand out of your beach towels and hang them up," Cousin Lou told them. "Then rinse your suits out in fresh water at the pump. It's going to be chowder and muffins and beachplum jam tonight. So march yourselves upstairs and write your Mother while I fix the chowder. She'll be anxious to hear from you. Time you're through, my muffins will be done. They only take twenty minutes." She glanced at her wrist, "Where do you suppose I left my watch?"

They looked around.

"Try and think when you had it last," suggested Peg. "That helps to remember."

"Now let me think...I had it this morning." Cousin Lou's face cleared. "Good for you, child. I remember now. Took it off when I set my pie to cool. Didn't want to get it wet in the dishpan. I put it on the window sill, right by the pie."

"Here goes," and Jeff dashed to the pantry. He came right back, shrugging his shoulders. "Not there," he reported. "Must have set it someplace else."

"No," said Cousin Lou. "I can recollect putting it there. Just a case of thinking back."

"We can ask Eric if he saw it, when he went for the pie," volunteered Peg.

"Eric! I'd clean forgotten him!" Cousin Lou's mouth set in a grim line. "I might have known! 'Like father, like son'!"

There was a terrible silence. Cousin Lou flushed. "Now whatever possessed me? Talk makes trouble. Forget what I said, you two. Put it out of your minds."

But Jeff had flushed to. "What you said is sort of hard to forget, Cousin Lou. Eric's our friend. He wouldn't take your watch!" He brightened. "We shared a locker at the beach house, and I hung our bluejeans on the same hook. Shook our pockets out, too, so our stuff wouldn't spill out. I put everything on the bench, and there wasn't any old watch, that's for sure!"

"We went by his house," Cousin Lou reminded him. "At his suggestion. He could have left it there."

Jeff and Peg looked at each other. "As long as you've said this much, you ought to tell the rest," insisted Jeff, even though Cousin Lou was glowering like a thunderhead.

"I've already expressed my regret for speaking out." Cousin Lou's voice was as sharp as a honed axe.

"Oh, Cousin Lou, it's not what you said!" exploded Peg. It's what you think! That's what matters. Why would Eric take your watch? Anyhow, what's his father got to do with it?"

"Well, if I've said this much I 'spose it should all be told. Only common fairness," sighed Cousin Lou. "Allan Clark and I were friends for years. Way back in third grade he carried my books home from school. Who'd expect him to do what he did?"

"What did he do?" urged Jeff. "That's what we want to know."

"I'll get to that. First, let's give him his due." She began ticking off on her fingers. "Ellistown's leading citizen. A Selectman, member of the school board, Town Improvement Committee. Busy as anything, but if anything needed tending to, Allan Clark took it on and got it done. He's some kind of scientist at the Woods Hole Oceanographic Institution, 'bout forty miles off. Lost his wife, some years back, but his sister Kate moved in, ran a neat house and tended the children. There are two girls a good bit older than Eric. Then, after the fire, everything changed." Cousin Lou sighed, and shook her head.

"What fire?" prodded Jeff. "When was it?"

"A year or so ago. At night. Allan Clark's barn burned clear to the ground."

"Too bad, but so what?" Jeff was mystified. "Fires happen every day. Why's this one such a big deal?"

Cousin Lou frowned. "Wonder if I can make you understand. Do you two know what insurance is?"

"I do!" boasted Peg. "One time Mom dented the car. She said she was glad it was insured, 'cause it wouldn't cost Dad any money."

"Let's make sure, though," urged Jeff. "You pay your money to the Insurance Company, and they can keep it unless something goes wrong. Is that it?"

"Yes," said Cousin Lou. "A man can insure his life. Or his car, or his barn. It protects him and his family from disaster. My watch isn't insured though. Wouldn't you know it?"

"How does the insurance company make money? I don't get that part," said Peg.

"Usually these calamities never happen," explained Cousin Lou. "I've carried fire insurance on my house for years, and never had to put in a claim." She tapped on wood. "Each year the company's collected and kept my small dribbles of money. It's been worth it to me for peace of mind. Once in a coon's age the company has to pay out. A lot more money than they took in, too. So of course they make sure the claim isn't false. They come 'round and ask questions."

"That figures," nodded Jeff. "Go on about Mr. Clark."

"Well, seems he took out a large fire insurance policy on his barn. Mind you, the big, fine house wasn't included. The policy only applied to the barn."

"What did he keep in his old barn?" asked Jeff. "Some kind of treasure?"

"You've put your finger right on it, Jeff. Allan Clark's a scientist, not a farmer. There wasn't one blessed thing kept in the barn except an old horse, and a few horse-show trophies. The trophies had no value at all, except sentimental. As for the horse, that caused more talk than anything else!"

"The <u>horse</u>?" asked Peg. "Why's that?"

"The horse was unharmed. He'd been let out before the fire started. Usually he's locked up for the night, but not this one time! Yet when Mr. Clark applied for the policy he told the insurance people that something very valuable was kept in the barn. He gave that as his reason for taking out such a large and expensive policy. When the barn burned down only <u>three</u> <u>weeks</u> later, you can't blame the company for wanting to investigate! They were going to have to pay out a lot of money to Mr. Clark!

"Well, what did they find?" asked Peg impatiently.

"Mr. Clark wouldn't permit the investigation," said Cousin Lou shortly. "He wouldn't let them set foot on the premises. Shoo'd off all his neighbors, too. We all tried to stand behind him, but he wasn't having any truck with any of us."

Jeff's eyebrows shot up. "Why not, for Pete's sake?"

"That's what everyone's asking," continued Cousin Lou. "Of course the insurance company refused to pay the claim. Can't say as I blame them!"

"Poor Mr. Clark! What did he do?" asked Peg.

"'Poor Mr. Clark' indeed! He resigned from the school committee within a week, and the Board of Selectmen too. Can't say what he's done about his job at Woods Hole. But he drives off toward Boston and stays five days a week. He only comes back here on weekends. His sister Kate's taken a job at the library, and the older girl looks after the house. Guess Eric looks after himself! They've cut loose from everything 'round here, and kept to themselves. Never explained a thing to anybody. Easy to guess what folks are saying..."

"That he set fire to an empty barn to collect the insurance money?" asked Jeff. "But that would be stealing!"

"Exactly." Cousin Lou sighed. "Now you know. Enough said. Too much, in fact. But I don't want that boy hanging 'round here. He's no longer welcome on these premises. Now go write those letters. I'll time my muffins by guess work."

Rooted to the spot, Jeff and Peg gazed sadly at each other. What Cousin Lou called "lollygagging". She looked at their forlorn little faces, and her heart ached for them.

"Come, come," she said, trying to make her voice bright. "Cheer up! Jeff, you can go up in the attic and bring down my gramophone, and my Stephen Foster records. I don't want any mourners at my feast. Tonight you're going to have your first quahog chowder!"

"Oh!" howled Peg. "<u>Eric's quahogs</u>!" She swallowed a sob and ran up the stairs.

Jeff followed her. Halfway up, he turned. "That's right, Cousin Lou," he said grimly. "Eric's quahogs. The ones he gave you. The ones you said <u>would fetch a good price at the fish pier</u>! And you say he stole your watch! It doesn't figure!"

Cousin Lou heaved a deep sign. "Whatever possessed me to talk so much? 'Least said, soonest mended!' Now I've gone and spoiled your day. I lay it at his father's door, but that boy's plain desperate for money. To begin with, he's got too much to do. He tends to half a dozen lawns for summer folks, and grooms horses at the big estates. Turns his hand to all sorts of odd jobs all over town, and does a man's work at home. He couldn't pass up a chance for easy money, right under his nose."

She looked stubbornly at Jeff's retreating back. "Keep your opinion, young man, and I'll hold to mine. Sure as Satan, that watch didn't walk off by itself."

CHAPTER FIVE

Jeff spent a wretched night. His black thoughts seemed to hang on the fragrant air like an ugly oil slick on the clear surface of a pool. Would he never get a good night's sleep? This time it wasn't the night noises that bothered him. He was unaware of them.

He kept thinking about Eric, and what Cousin Lou had told them about Eric's father. Jeff squirmed, remembering how he and Peg had complained about their few chores. Eric had mountains of real work to do, and all those troubles, and the whole town turned against his family, and a crying need for money. He had enough to bear without being called a thief! What would happen if Eric came over to Cousin Lou's? She'd be sure to turn him away, and give him a piece of her mind, with her sharp tongue! What was it Mom had said? That Cousin Lou's mind couldn't be changed with a bulldozer! What could he and Peg do to straighten things out? His thoughts raced round and round, and for what seemed like hours, he couldn't come up with a thing.

At six o'clock the next morning, when it seemed to Jeff that he'd barely gotten to sleep, he heard a light tap on his door, and Peg stuck her head in.

"Shh!" she whispered. "We've got to talk. Are you awake enough? You sure don't look it!"

"No wonder! I stayed awake most of the night. I kept hearing Cousin Lou." Jeff mimicked her clipped

50

New England twang. "'That watch couldn't walk off by itself!'"

"Jeff!" Peg glared at him. "Are you saying…"

"Of course not, silly." Jeff didn't even let her finish. "That's it. We know Eric didn't take it. So who else? We've got to find out, or Cousin Lou'll go right on thinking Eric's a thief. Sooner or later he'll hear about it, and that's too awful to think about! 'Bout midnight I slipped downstairs for a snack, and got this crazy idea. Now I need a chance to test it."

"Tell me! I stayed awake for ages too. Couldn't think of a single thing." Peg bounced up and down on his bed.

Jeff shook his head. "I'm not ready to talk about it."

"And leave me out? No fair!" Peg raised her voice.

"Quiet or you'll wake Cousin Lou! You can help later."

"When?" asked Peg. "That's what I came up about. We told Eric we'd meet him at the Salt Pond at ten, remember? How are we going to manage it? Cousin Lou'd have a fit. She doesn't even want us to see him anymore!"

"Simple. We do our chores, then go off on our own, the way she said we could. No need to say anything. This afternoon, though, I need some time to myself. That's where you come in. Can you manage to get Cousin Lou off the place?"

Peg wrinkled her forehead. "Got it! Remember that folder about things for tourists to do on Cape Cod? There was one of the back of every seat on the Bonanza bus. It told about a famous Doll Museum at a town called Sandwich. Maybe I could get her to take me."

"Great. You get it fixed up, and when we're leaving, I'll duck it. Now go on back to your room before she gets up. I know one thing! Cousin Lou doesn't lie around in bed very late!"

Peg couldn't help laughing at the idea of bustling Cousin Lou lolling in bed much after six o'clock. "Don't forget what Eric told us," she reminded her brother. "Wear your bathing suit under your blue jeans." She tiptoed out.

As Jeff had foretold, getting away to the Salt Pond posed no problem. What they saw when they got there made their eyes pop.

Eric had launched a small, flat-bottomed skiff. Inside was a queer machine, and he was bending over it.

"Hurrah! Glad you two made it. I need you. Now I can start up this diesel engine."

Jeff and Peg peeled off their sweatshirt and blue jeans. "What's that contraption?" asked Jeff, as they waded out to the skiff. They peered inside. Something that looked like an oversize vacuum cleaner was on the bottom. A long ankle-thick hose ran from it to another weird piece, which looked like a giant pair of barber's shears. A cord connected the strange machine to the diesel.

"Watch out!" yelled Eric. "Here goes!" He heaved the heavy shears into the pond. There was a mighty splash. Eric's boat rocked dangerously, and ripples raced toward shore in ever-widening circles. Dead silence followed. Jeff and Peg were speechless.

Eric beamed. "There goes Dad's handiest invention!"

Jeff recovered his voice. "Have you flipped, or something? What'll your dad say? Why did you do that, and what are you going to do with it?"

Eric was smiling mischievously. "I'm not going to do a thing with it. You are. I've made two trips from home, lugging all this stuff in a wheelbarrow, and I'm pooped. I'll stay here high and dry, and follow you 'round with the boat. You two sure look good to me!"

"What do we do?" asked Jeff doubtfully.

"Push the shears around on the bottom, like a regular lawnmower. You can manage that, can't you?"

"Guess so. If you don't go out too deep!"

"The water's only up to your waist, for Pete's sake! When I throw the switch, lean on the handles and push. Start round the edge of the pond, in the very shallow water."

Jeff and Peg grabbed on to the handles.

"Hold on!" shouted Eric. He threw the switch, and they pushed hard. The machine began to move

53

across the bottom. The hose shivered like a live thing, and grew taut. It was evident that something was being sucked into the boat. Jeff and Peg were too busy keeping their footing on the oozy bottom to see what.

An hour later, they had almost completed their circle of the pond. Suddenly the shears hit something solid, raising a sheet of spray and coming to a full stop. Jeff and Peg were both pitched forward by the impact.

"Ouch!" Jeff rubbed his ribs. "You okay, Peg?"

"Guess so. My shoulder hurts, though. What did we hit, a rock? It felt like a stone wall!"

Jeff leaned over to investigate. "It's a barrel!" he yelled. "A big round barrel bound with metal strips." He bent over and pushed against it. "It won't budge!"

"Leave it alone," called Eric. "We'll tie a rope around it and let the boat haul it ashore."

Now that they were no longer pushing, Jeff and Peg turned around and looked back at him. Only his head was visible. The whole boat was full of wet, slimy moss.

"What? You mean we worked ourselves loop-legged and nearly got killed, just to smooth off the bottom of your old pond? What are you going to do with that awful stuff?"

Eric laughed so hard he nearly fell overboard. "That 'awful stuff' is sea-moss, and it's worth money.

We'll have to spread it out on the shore to dry in the sun. Later, we'll pile it into wind-rows."

"What's it for?" Peg found it hard to believe anyone could use the slimy, evil-smelling moss.

"Oh, lots of things. Bet you've eaten 'bout a ton of it yourself."

"Me? Eat that? Not for a million dollars!"

"Give up ice-cream and pudding, then," said Eric cheerfully. "Sea-moss is used in gelatin, and gelatin goes into ice-cream. Back in the old days folks used it to insulate their houses. Bet Miss Bowman's old walls are crammed with it. That's not all. Florists use sea-moss for packing cut flowers. It's used in medicines, too, and I don't know what all. This load's worth a lot of money, and my Dad could sure use some of that!" Eric stopped short. "Say, what's the matter with me? You ought to get paid for all the work you did. Couldn't have done it alone, and I can't count on Dad for any help these days."

Jeff was dying to ask why, but thought better of it.

"We don't want to get paid," he protested. "When will we ever get another chance to do something like this? Wait until I tell my friends back home that I'm a sea farmer!" He looked puzzled. "Yesterday you said Old Joe taught you how to sea-farm. Where would that old guy get machinery like this?"

"He taught me to do it by hand," explained Eric. "It would have taken us 'bout a week to haul in what we did this morning. Awhile back, this was a big industry 'round here, but it kind of died out. Took too much

55

time, and too many people. Then Dad got interested. He dreamed up a simple way to do the job."

Jeff looked at Eric. "Honestly! You're like an encyclopedia, only a lot more fun! Why, I've only known you about 24 hours, and already you're one of my best friends."

"Same with me." Eric paused. "Say, maybe next summer you two can come and stay at my house, in case Miss Bowman doesn't ask you back. We'd really stir up some action! Meantime, I've gotten Dad going on the clambake. Tonight at six o'clock on the beach behind these dunes. Dad goes back to Boston in the morning, so it's got to be tonight."

Jeff managed a nod, but he didn't dare look at Peg. "Come on," he urged. "Let's haul in the barrel and see what's inside."

Eric tossed him a rope. "Loop that around it with a slip-knot. Then I'll start my motor and move ahead in low gear. That ought to loosen it, and we can roll it ashore."

When they had rolled the barrel up to a dry spot, they couldn't open it.

"It's nailed up tight," said Eric. "We'll have to pry off the lid."

"What with?" Peg looked around the deserted beach.

"There's a screwdriver in my tool kit. Look in the wheelbarrow."

When they finally got the lid off they had to scoop out several layers of seaweed. Eric stuck his arm down inside and pulled out a bulky, burlap-wrapped bundle. "What do you reckon this is?" he muttered. "Somebody sure packed it for keeps! It's bone-dry."

"Hurry up!" Jeff and Peg were nearly popping.

"Maybe it's pirate's loot," said Peg.

"In this modern barrel?" Eric was trying to keep calm. He overturned the barrel, spilling out several other well-wrapped bundles. "Let's each take one, and open them up together."

Feverishly their fingers scrabbled with the wrappings. Then Eric held up a gleaming loving-cup. He seemed dumbfounded.

"Silver! I told you it was pirate's loot!" yelled Peg. "Look! I've got another one!"

"Same here," said Jeff. "Three of them."

"Pirate's loot, my foot," said Jeff savagely. "Those are horse show trophies. See, here's my name on this one. My sisters won most of the others."

"Then what are they doing on the bottom of Salt Pond?" asked Jeff. "Who'd put them there?"

Eric didn't answer. Jeff glanced at his friend and saw raw pain etched on his face. His eyes were so sad that instinctively Jeff turned his own away.

"How long do you 'spose they've been there?" asked Peg, who hadn't looked up.

"I can tell you that much. Since just before our fire. That was a year ago," Eric explained. "I figured the trophies had burned up in the barn. Where they were kept..."

"Then the thief had to steal them before the fire," said Jeff. "That much is clear."

Eric scowled. "Yep," he said shortly. "Crystal clear."

"If he bothered to steal them, why sink them in the pond?" insisted Jeff. "Why didn't he sell them?"

"They're only plated. Not worth much to anyone but Dad. He's no horseman and he's proud of my sisters. They've won all the big shows 'round here." Eric scratched his head. "I was in that barn every single day. If that trophy shelf had been empty, I'd have noticed it, that's for sure. They were right there clear up until the fire!" He piled them into the wheelbarrow.

"Look, kids," he said gruffly, "I've got to beat it. Got to straighten something out with my Dad. Right away."

Again Jeff avoided looking at Peg. "We ought to mosey on home too," he said. "We didn't tell Cousin Lou where we were headed."

"I need to keep busy this afternoon," said Eric. He scowled. "No use sitting 'round with my thoughts. What'll we do?"

"Cousin Lou's taking us sightseeing," said Jeff. "Some old Doll Museum Peg wants to see. Sounds awful."

"Oh. Guess you can count me out. I've been dragged there once, and that's enough dolls for me. See you tonight at the clambake, though. Tomorrow morning, too. Same time. Want me to come by your place?"

"Tell you what," hastened Jeff. "We'd a lot rather keep clear of Cousin Lou. So let's meet at the head of the lane on old Nelly. She owes us a ride after all the hay I hauled for her this morning. Come over on your own horse."

"Okay. I'll ride over on Whitefoot. But how did you know I have a horse?"

Jeff swallowed. "I figured you would. The trophies, and everything. See you!"

As he and Peg walked back to Cousin Lou's, Jeff looked miserable and tired. "What a problem!" he groaned.

"Which one?" asked Peg. "Too many to keep track of."

"Well, the clambake, for a start. Cousin Lou's never in a million years going to let us go. She won't let us have anything to do with any of the Clarks. How'll we every explain that to Eric? He's getting the whole blast up just for us. Six o'clock's long before sunset, we can't possibly slip away from the house. What can we do?"

"Everything's getting all mixed up!" sighed Peg. "You nearly spilled the beans, smarty! You nearly gave away that Cousin Lou had already told us about the fire, and about Eric's horse that was outside when the barn burned..."

"I know. I had to think fast." Jeff looked unhappy. "Keep your fingers crossed! Cousin Lou mustn't hear about our finding those trophies, and one thing's sure. She doesn't miss much! Those trophies <u>prove</u> the fire wasn't an accident. I wish we'd never gone near Salt Pond! Know what we did today? <u>We</u> <u>nailed</u> <u>down</u> <u>the</u> <u>case</u> <u>against</u> <u>Eric's</u> <u>dad</u>!" His voice broke.

"How do you figure that?" asked Peg.

"Are you dumb, or something?" In his heartache for his friend, Jeff spoke roughly. "Nobody else gave a hoot about those old trophies. Eric told us so himself! Mr. Clark must have stashed them in a safe place before firing off the barn. Didn't you hear Eric say his father needs money?"

"Why would he go to all that bother? asked Peg. "All he had to do was move the trophies into his house..."

"Nobody could be that stupid!" Jeff's tone was elaborately patient. "Remember, the barn was empty except for the trophies and the horse. Mr. Clark let the horse out! If he'd saved the trophies too, it would have looked phony as a three dollar bill. It was better to hide them. In a few years he'd haul them out. By then nobody would remember they're supposed to be all burned up. It was a perfect plan until we wrecked it. They'd already been sitting in the pond for a year!" Jeff kicked viciously at a stone.

They walked along, dragging their feet. Jeff couldn't stop tormenting himself. "Did you see Eric's face?" he groaned. "He's figured it out! In fact it came right up and hit him in the face, same as me. What could be worse?"

Peg stopped short. "Oh no, Jeff! That's too awful…" She swallowed hard. "His own father…And we helped…You don't know for sure…"

"I don't know anything!" Jeff was close to tears. "Except one thing. We need to watch every single word we say to everybody. We're caught right in the middle." He groaned. "It's awful, having to deceive them all…Cousin Lou…Eric. What else can we do?"

They walked along awhile in grim silence. "You said we have a problem, Jeff," sighed Peg. "Wish we did have only one. We might manage that. But how can we possibly handle a ton of them, all by ourselves?"

Jeff stopped short. He eyed her anxiously. "Cut that out, Peg!" he told her sharply. "We've got to find a way to help Eric. It's us or nobody." He took her hand. "Come on, cheer up. We'll be facing Cousin Lou at lunch in about five minutes! Don't look so worried or she'll wise up!"

"Don't I know it! She's got eyes that look right through us. Right now I'd rather be having lunch with 'most anybody, anywhere!"

"With the school principal, in his office?" teased Jeff, eager to divert her.

"Any day!" In spite of herself Peg brightened. "I'd rather be out in the pasture having lunch with Eric's horse!"

"That wouldn't be so bad," said Jeff. "How's this? I'd rather be down at the beach having lunch with Old Joe in that filthy old shack?" Laughing, they walked into Cousin Lou's kitchen.

"Here you are!" she said. "About time, too. Five more minutes and you'd have missed out on fresh swordfish and cranberry pudding." She eyed them closely. "You two look as though butter wouldn't melt in your mouths. If I didn't know how quiet things are in these parts, I'd vow you two'd been up to something!"

CHAPTER SIX

Cousin Lou rinsed the dishes and stacked them neatly in the sink. "These can wait," she said. "Afternoon's too beautiful to waste, and it's a long drive to Sandwich. Run fetch a sweater, Peg. As for you, Jeff, your hair could stand a comb. Step lively, now."

"Oh thanks, Cousin Lou!" said Peg with a straight face. "If you only knew how much I want to see those dolls!"

Jeff shuffled his feet. "Tell you what, Cousin Lou, there are things I'd rather do right here."

Cousin Lou nodded understandingly. "I 'spose so. A Doll Museum's no place for an active boy. This afternoon will be Peg's treat. I'll make it up to you later, Jeff. I'll try to take you aboard the <u>Atlantis</u>."

Jeff rose to the bait like a trout to the fly. "The <u>Atlantis</u>? What's that?"

"A special ship provided to the Oceanographic Institution by the National Science Foundation. The oceanographers use it for exploration of the sea. It's full of all the latest scientific equipment. Don't set your heart on it, though. We'd need a permit, and I'm not sure I could wrangle one."

"Couldn't you ask Mr. Clark?" blurted Jeff, without taking time to think.

"I don't hold with begging favors, least of all from him," said Cousin Lou curtly.

Peg took a deep breath. "Speaking of Mr. Clark, he's invited us to a clambake tonight, on the beach behind Salt Pond. Isn't that exciting? We've never had a chance to go to one."

"And you're not going on this one!" said Cousin Lou firmly. "You know why as well's I do. While you're in my charge I won't have you associating with either Eric or his father. That boy took my watch as sure as anything. He's queered himself with me for keeps. A leopard doesn't change its spot!"

Jeff didn't give up. "But it's all planned, Cousin Lou. All that work getting things ready, and all that food going to waste!"

Something like a grim smile hovered around Cousin Lou's mouth. "That will give Allan Clark a dose of his own medicine," she declared. "Someday I'll tell you about the barn raising the neighbors staged for him two days after his big fire."

"What on earth's a barn raising?" asked Peg.

"An old New England custom that's persisted. Dates back to early times. If a man lost his barn in this climate it spelled disaster. Whole town would come to his rescue. Minister, bank president, Mayor, everybody. They'd all come with their tools and before sundown they'd raise the ridgepole. Then there'd be fiddling and dancing and feasting on all the good things the women brought, like home baked beans and pies and such…"

"Sounds like a real blast," said Jeff. "Is that what Ellistown folks did for Mr. Clark?"

"It's what they tried to do. I have a light hand with doughnuts and I made four dozen of them myself. Took along six jars of my spiced peaches too. Nobody came empty-handed. Some of the men had lost a day's pay to be there and lend a hand."

"Did you get the ridgepole raised?" asked Jeff.

"We did not. Allan Clark and his sister Kate were standing at the front door when we pulled up. They looked might uncomfortable, I will say that for them. Thanked us ever so nicely for our trouble. Said they weren't sure about what kind of barn to rebuild and that they 'preferred to wait'. A likely story!"

"Couldn't it have been true?" asked Peg.

Cousin Lou snorted. "Nobody looks a gift horse in the mouth. The labor and material being offered them for free was worth hundreds of dollars. The goodwill was worth more. Nobody turns away forty people carrying home cooked food, either. Anyhow, it was a perfect summer day and we could at least have had a picnic on the lawn. Some of the ladies were already unloading the beachwagons. Then Miss Kate said something about it's not being a convenient time. In other words, we weren't welcome!" She set her mouth in a grim line.

"Then what?" asked Jeff faintly, mentally saying goodbye to any lingering hopes for the clambake.

"Everybody packed up in a hurry and left. Mad as hornets, too. So don't expect me to cry over the wasted food at Allan Clark's outing. I've never crossed his gate-posts from that day to this, and I don't reckon anybody else in the village has either." She glanced up at the sun. "Time's getting by while I stand here raking over old coals. Wish we could forget about the Clarks! Come along now, Peg. Step lively. Think you can fend for yourself, boy?"

"I'll try, Cousin Lou." Jeff spoke so seriously that Peg had to turn away to hide a grin.

When the old jeep turned out into the road, backfiring as it climbed the grade, Jeff heaved a sigh of relief. Peg had certainly pulled that one off! He had to hand it to her. Now he ought to be able to count on about three hours to do his sleuthing. It might be the only chance he'd ever get.

He ran out to the stable, gave old Nelly's nose a pat, and found the ladder he'd spied earlier. He dragged it out, raising a cloud of dust, then hauled it clear across the lawn. He managed to prop it directly under the big elm tree next to his bedroom window. The ladder was a long one, but it came a few feet short of the lower branches.

Jeff kicked off his shoes and climbed to the top rung. He stood up on tiptoes and gave a mighty leap. At the very moment that his hands closed around a branch, he heard a crash. His big leap had tipped over the ladder!

His fingers gripped the limb convulsively, but he felt them beginning to slip. They were holding the full weight of his swinging body and the rugged bark bit sharply into them. His shoulders were being jerked from their sockets! Quickly he swung his dangling feet against the tree trunk and managed to ease the tension on his shoulders and to scramble up far enough to throw one leg over the branch. He was gasping and panting like a shipwrecked sailor clinging to a reef and he could feel his heart knocking against his chest. He had to stay there and catch his breath before he could haul himself up the rest of the way and straddle the sturdy limb.

Now for the first time he dared to look down. The ground seemed a long way off. Even if he could muster up the nerve to jump, he might land on the ladder and sprain an ankle, or worse. It looked like a long afternoon's roost in the elm tree! But it would be worth it, if only his crazy idea paid off.

He climbed further up the tree, placing each foot carefully and taking his time, to a place where the trunk forked off. There in the crotch he saw a dark hole. He took a deep breath, screwed up his courage, and plunged his arm in…down, down, through dead leaves and twigs, almost to his shoulder. His fingers fastened on something long and hard. He grabbed hold of it and pulled it out.

"What on earth…" he muttered. He held it up to the light and turned it over. He thrust it into his pocket, disgusted. He certainly hadn't come up here for that! He worked his arm back into the hole and found nothing more. He climbed right to the top of the tree, his disappointment mounting as he rose. Finally he inched himself back to the lower limb and settled himself as best he could, leaning against the trunk and hooking his feet around the branch so as not to topple over. He hadn't accomplished a thing! He'd wasted his whole afternoon, and now he'd have to wait for the others to get back. Even the Doll Museum would have been better than this. How he wished he'd spent the afternoon with Eric, instead of on this wild goose chase!

When Cousin Lou and Peg pulled into the driveway over two hours later Jeff hailed them eagerly.

"What in tarnation?" Cousin Lou spied the ladder on the ground and guessed what had happened. She put her hands on her hips and tilted her head upward. "Should have had better sense than to leave you behind. Boys and trouble just naturally go together. Been stranded long?"

"Ever since about ten minutes after you left," Jeff admitted.

"A crying shame! Here, Peg, give me a hand." Together they lifted up the ladder, and both of them braced it firmly against the tree. Jeff scrambled down, rubbing his stiff joints.

"A pity you didn't come along," said Cousin Lou. "Such a wasted afternoon for you!"

"Not exactly, Cousin Lou."

"I don't hold with idleness." Cousin Lou frowned. "That's not saying it was your fault, Jeff, and nobody's blaming you. One whole afternoon gone, though, and not a blessed thing to show for it."

"How 'bout this?" Jeff pulled something out of his pocket and dangled it before her eyes. It glinted in the late afternoon sun.

"My coin silver spoon!" cried Cousin Lou. "One of them vanished weeks ago. Ruined my set, and my disposition too. Thought I'd thrown it out in the trash can. Wherever did you find it, boy?"

"In the thieves' hiding place," said Jeff.

"Thieves!" Cousin Lou turned pale. "And here you were, all alone. Lucky to escape them up that tree!"

But Peg was bouncing up and down like a yoyo. "Good for you, Jeff. Rascal and Bandit! How'd you think of them?"

"Remember the big fuss they made, the night we got here? Well, late last night they started up again, and I remembered what Cousin Lou told us. About their clever fingers. I figured maybe they'd taken her watch. That's what I was looking for, not an old spoon. Didn't even know one was missing. How'd they get hold of it?"

"Sometimes I eat my lunch beneath the elm tree," said Cousin Lou. "Must have dropped it there. They like shiny things."

"How about the watch, though?" asked Peg. "Was it up there too, Jeff? The watch is what's important."

"Nope. I looked everywhere. Even poked my hand down into a hollow, way up there near the tip top." He craned his neck and pointed. "The hole was full of dead leaves. Rascal and Bandit's bed, I guess.

Lucky for me they weren't in it. I'd have dropped dead! That's where the spoon was. No watch, though."

"Oh well," said Cousin Lou. "I'm thankful to get the spoon back. I never expect to see that watch again." She sighed. "It was my mother's. That watch is worth a lot to me."

"It is worth a whole pie, all for me?" asked Jeff. "Oh, I might give Peg a bite or two," he added grandly.

"Thought you said it wasn't up there!" Peg accused him. "Did you really find it?"

"Not yet, but I'm about to." Jeff ran over to the rhododendron bush just below the kitchen window sill, thrust his arm down, and then withdrew it.

"Here you are, Cousin Lou. Guess it fell off the window ledge when Eric grabbed up the pie, then got caught in the bush before it hit the ground. I wouldn't have seen it in a million years if I hadn't had that long roost right directly above it in the elm tree. I looked straight down on it, and nearly fell off! Looks as good as new. Hasn't been rained on, or anything."

Cousin Lou held the watch to her ear. "It hasn't even run down. I'm right glad to get it back!" She cleared her throat. "No need to waste words saying I'm ashamed of having called Eric a thief. Wish I could un-say those words. I'm a stubborn old fool, that what! What's done's done, though. Not a blessed thing I can do about it."

"Oh Cousin Lou," exclaimed Peg. "There is! There really is!"

"Is what?" asked Jeff. "What are you talking about, anyhow?"

"There is something Cousin Lou could do about it," Peg insisted stubbornly. "If only she would!"

"Speak your piece, child," said Cousin Lou. "Listening never hurt anybody."

CHAPTER SEVEN

Now that the spotlight was on her, Peg seemed to be having a hard time expressing her thought.

"It's like this," she began. "Way back in second grade, the teacher said that <u>3 plus 1 makes 4</u>. Then she told us to put it backwards. You get the same answer!"

"So what!" scoffed Jeff. "Everybody knows that! What's that supposed to prove?"

Cousin Lou laid a restraining hand on his sleeve. "Go on, Peg," she urged. "Make your point."

"Well, when you thought Eric was a thief, you said 'Like father, like son'. So why wouldn't it work backwards, same as arithmetic? 'Like son, like father'?"

"I get it!" Jeff broke in. "You don't know for sure that Mr. Clark did anything wrong, now do you, Cousin Lou? It only looks that way. Same's with Eric."

Cousin Lou bit her lip and considered. "Can't say as I have any proof," she conceded. "I didn't <u>see</u> him set fire to his barn...and I'm right shaken up by the way I misjudged Eric. I 'spose it's possible. Anyhow, a whole year's gone by. It's too late..."

"Wait a minute!" said Peg. "Driving down here, Mr. Clark was telling us how oceanographers collect clues from the ocean floor. To help figure out what happened ages ago. Maybe we can do the same thing…study the clues!"

"Do we have any?" Cousin Lou sounded doubtful.

"Let's go back to the starting point and begin with the barn," urged Jeff. "What do we know about it?"

"Only that it was empty, except for Whitefoot and his sacks of oats and a few trophies," said Cousin Lou. "Been like that for years.

"As far as you know. But Mr. Clark said it contained something valuable," Jeff reminded her. "Ever known him to tell a lie?"

"No," Cousin Lou admitted. "Can't say's I have."

"And a leopard doesn't change its spots." Peg couldn't resist reminding her.

"Know what?" Jeff broke in. "Seems to me you and all the folks in Ellistown were in such a flap about being turned away from the barn raising that you didn't give him half a chance. Why don't we figure he was telling the truth? There <u>was</u> something valuable in his own barn."

In spite of herself, Cousin Lou was getting interested. "Not money. Hasn't got much, and anyhow, he's no miser."

"Does it matter?" asked Jeff. "We don't really need to know. The point is, he wouldn't want to lose it if he valued it…"

"So he wouldn't want the barn to catch fire!" interrupted Peg.

"I get your point and it's a good one," said Cousin Lou. "But why did he send the investigator away? What was there to hide? That's what lost him the insurance money that was due him. For that matter, why did he offend all his neighbors who were trying to stand by him? He's no fool! He knew what he was doing! Know what I think? He didn't dare risk anybody poking around his premises!"

"You're still getting things backwards, Cousin Lou! Don't you see?" Jeff was so excited that his voice cracked. "If he'd burned down his barn on purpose to gyp the insurance company, he would have <u>expected</u> a visit from their investigator. He'd have welcomed him, not turned him away!"

Cousin Lou put both hands up to her ears. "I don't rightly know what's what! You two have got me all mixed up. The way you tell it, Allan Clark would have welcomed the investigator if he'd set the fire. But there was no sense in <u>not</u> welcoming him if he was innocent! The whole thing's as tangled as the wool in my yarn basket!"

All three of them thought a while.

"Seems to me we've come up against a blank wall," signed Cousin Lou.

But Jeff wasn't ready to give up. "Let's stick to what we know, or we'll get off track. It's a fact that he <u>did</u> turn the guy away. What would make him do that? What reason could be strong enough to make him throw away thousands of dollars?"

"Can't think of any," said Cousin Lou. "Minds as blank as a washed slate. Peg, any thoughts to add?"

Peg shook her head. "How 'bout you, Jeff? Got any ideas?"

"Just one." Jeff frowned. "It's still kind of fuzzy and I haven't finished working it out." His face cleared. "Yep. It's got to be that! It's just got to!" He groaned. "I don't have all the facts, and I can't read Mr. Clark's mind! There are things I need to know. How'm I ever going to find them out?"

"That's easy," said Peg. "You can ask him."

There was a moment of stunned silence. Then Cousin Lou cleared her throat and nodded vigorously.

"She's dead right, Jeff," she said. "It's what I should have done a year ago. Instead, I let pride and a batch of doughnuts stand in the way.

Now get moving, you two! No time to waste, because Allan Clark goes back to Boston tomorrow. Shake a leg and don't stand there gaping! <u>We're going to a clambake</u>!"

CHAPTER EIGHT

Peg and Jeff came tumbling out the front door, sweaters and beach towels trailing behind them like kite tails. They raced for the jeep. Cousin Lou, face as puckered as a persimmon, was standing guard beside it. "What's a body got legs for?" she grumbled. "Less than a mile! We walk!"

The two of them skipped ahead, undaunted. How was she supposed to know they'd already make the whole round trip on foot that very morning? Anyhow, they were getting used to Cousin Lou. "She's all nerved up," said Peg when they were out of earshot. "Her bark's worse than her bite."

Jeff choked back a whoop. "You're beginning to sound just like her," he teased. "Can't wait to see Mom's face when you come out with 'Waste not, want not', and 'A stitch in time saves nine'! You're really going to fracture the fifth grade!"

But Peg wouldn't let herself be sidetracked. "Maybe so. But most of what Cousin Lou says makes sense. It's only the way she says it...sort of like a snapping turtle. Anyhow, you can't fool me. You're kind of nerved up yourself, and I know why. You're not really sure of anything, are you Jeff? This morning you were positive those sunken trophies proved the case against Eric's dad. Tonight you've got a new idea. They can't both be right. So which one is? We might not <u>like</u> the answers to all our questions! And Eric's going to be right on hand to hear them. Had you thought of that?"

Jeff's stomach did a flip-flop. He looked so shaken that Peg could have pinched herself. She wished she'd kept her mouth shut. Jeff needed all his confidence and all his courage, and now he was looking as deflated as a pricked balloon! What was it Cousin Lou was fond of saying? 'Least said, soonest mended.' Well, it was true!

They kept on walking, and soon Cousin Lou caught up with them. On impulse, Peg grabbed her hand and squeezed it, and instantly Cousin Lou went through one of her weather changes. She could veer up like a compass in a spring wind!

"Buck up, you two!" she urged them kindly. "You're headed for a feast, not a firing squad!"

They quickened their pace and The evening sun, brassy yellow and backlighting seagrass of an almost blinding green was sparkling like mica on Salt Pond. They breathed deeply, smelling the salt air and the bracken and the rose mallows, and hearing the sleepy twittering of the birds in the marsh and the soft swoosh of ocean waves, regular and gentle, behind the dunes. A wedge of Canadian geese, honking wildly and flying in formation, passed directly across the sun. It was impossible not to feel better. All three of them looked at each other. They smiled and squared their shoulders and felt like a team. "It's always fair weather when we all pull together," said Cousin Lou, and this time they didn't feel like laughing at her.

They scrambled up the dunes and looked down. The first sight to greet their eyes was the protruding metal rim of a great sunken barrel. From it rose a cloud of fragrant steam that fanned and feathered into soft streamers in the southwest breeze. Allan Clark, his back to them, was poking at the hot stones lining the hut. At Eric's welcoming shout he straightened up and turned around. Sheer astonishment made him speechless.

"Land's sakes!" exclaimed a jolly looking lady, as plump as a cupcake. "Look what the tide's brought in! Lou, you're the cherry on the pudding. Nobody thought you'd come."

"We weren't even sure you'd send Jeff and Peg," said Mr. Clark. "I've been trying my best to brace Eric for the disappointment."

"Left to myself I'd have kept my distance." Cousin Lou was never going to be mistaken for a diplomat. "These kids put me up to it. I'm putty in their hands."

"Funny. We never noticed," said Jeff, trying to keep his face straight.

"Don't be too big for your britches, young man!" But Cousin Lou wasn't really paying him much mind. She was thinking about what she'd come to say and hear.

"You and I have got a lot to straighten out, Allan. Sooner the better."

"Aren't you about a year late, Lou?" Allan Clark had stiffened visibly.

"If it's waited a whole year, couldn't it wait until after supper." Peg asked anxiously.

"Of course it could." Miss Kate stepped into the breach. "Lou, maybe you'd melt the butter, then mix the salad greens. I'm right glad for an extra pair of hands! Set out my doughnuts, too. They're not as light as yours," she added generously.

Cousin Lou began to look a lot more mellow. She set a pan of butter on the sand abutting the hot stones. A drift of smoke wafted toward her and she sniffed appreciatively. "Nothing beats a clambake for good smells. Glad we came."

"Oh, we are too, Miss Bowman!" Eric spoke so fervently that all the grown-ups smiled, and the party was off to a good start.

Eric had contrived a makeshift table from planks set on stones, and Peg laid out the things that were handed to her. "Bibs!" she exclaimed. "Never expected to wear another. Guess we'll need them, though. Nutcrackers and picks, too. A lot more fun that forks and knives."

"Lobsters are armor plated," Eric told her. "Or it seems that way. Wait until you try opening one. Dad can do it with exactly four flicks of his wrist. Even the claws."

His father added, "Something we learned years ago from Old Joe, didn't we Lou? He rowed us out to his lobster pots, then hauled them in and cooked the lobsters on this very beach. We must have been around seven, and Kate was nine."

79

Peg couldn't help nudging Jeff. It was hard to realize that Cousin Lou had ever been seven years old. She seemed timeless, part of the landscape, like an old tree or her weathered Cape Cod house.

"I'm starting the countdown," warned Mr. Clark. "Ready, get set, go! But don't forget to pace yourselves. That barrel holds a lot!"

First each person was given a bowl filled to the brim with steamers, and his own smaller bowl of melted butter.

"Well, I never!" Jeff exclaimed. "These clams are open! I thought we'd have to crack them. Like the gulls."

"Gulls can't light fires," Miss Kate reminded him. "Heat steams the clam's shells apart. All you need to do is pull it out, dunk it in butter and pop it in your mouth. Chances are, you'll come back for another round."

She was right. Next they each had two lobsters, along with several sweet potatoes and too many ears of corn to count. Then Miss Kate cut thick half-moons of watermelon. "Doughnut, anybody? Or shall we wait awhile?"

Jeff stretched out a butter-smeared hand. "I'll tackle it." He sighed blissfully. "Might make me pop, but can you think of a better way to go!"

When they had finished, and carefully collected their refuse, they packaged it to take home. Next they doused seawater on the hot stones, enjoying the hiss and the surging clouds of steam. The sun, now dark red, had almost reached the horizon. It lingered there a moment and then it disappeared, swallowed whole, creating the optical illusion that it had been engulfed into the sea. A rosy afterglow began to streak across the sky.

"The night has a thousand eyes, and the day but one, and yet the whole world dies, when dies the sun," quoted Cousin Lou.

"What a surprising person you are, Lou. Who'd have expected you to quote poetry? And so aptly." Allan Clark burrowed a little hollow in the sand, settled himself down in it and lit his pipe. "Perhaps each of us has his hidden side."

"It's about yours that we came over." Cousin Lou, who'd been melting like ice cream in the oven, seemed to take a mental hitch on herself. "Time's past for beating 'round the bush. Might as well come to the point."

"You always did." Miss Kate spoke dryly.

"Why don't we turn it into a game? You know, like Twenty Questions?" Peg was desperately trying to keep alive the good feelings engendered by the feast. "Let Jeff start!"

"Here goes." Jeff swallowed hard. "Mr. Clark, what did you keep in your barn? Besides Whitefoot and the trophies?"

"Do you know, Jeff, you're the only person who's asked me that in a whole year! And what a long year it's been! Don't ever talk to me about time flying!"

"Nobody but yourself to blame!" snorted Cousin Lou. "Whole town came rushing over, soon's word got round that you had trouble on your hands. Got shunted off like the plague for our trouble!"

"I know, Lou. Don't think Kate and I haven't gone over it a hundred times. You took us by surprise. I couldn't have the men go near the barn."

"Isn't that exactly what I told you, Jeff?" Cousin Lou shot him a triumphant look. "That he didn't want folks pokin' round his premises?"

Jeff paid her no heed. "Why not? That takes us right back to my question, sir. What was in the barn? Or maybe you don't want to say. We don't really have a right to ask!"

"After what you kids did this morning, you've got every right," said Allan Clark, and Cousin Lou looked mystified. "Because of that, I can talk about it. I had an invention in the barn. An important one. The model was almost finished when the barn burned."

"Odd place to keep it," said Cousin Lou.

"Not at all. The empty barn was ideal for my purposes. No kids underfoot, no noise. I took over the empty loft, moved in a desk and a drafting board and all my tools, and set to work every moment I could spare from my regular jobs at Woods Hole."

"Tell us about the invention," urged Jeff.

"We have a long-term project under way at the Oceanographic," Mr. Clark told him. "To map the floor of all the world's oceans. Those oceans cover three quarters of our planet!"

"Wow! How do you map them?" Jeff asked eagerly.

"We make expeditions on the <u>Atlantis</u>. We take depth soundings, by using sonar."

"What's sonar?" Peg wanted to know.

"An electronic instrument that bounces sound off the seafloor, then times the return. That gives us the depth. It's remarkably accurate, but our big problem is the expense involved."

"To you?" Cousin Lou seemed surprised.

"Not to me, Lou. To the Oceanographic. The expense of operating the <u>Atlantis</u>. More than twenty thousand dollars <u>a day</u>!"

"Zowie!" Jeff whistled.

"Our Institution is world famous, but it's small. With such high costs, we can't run as many <u>Atlantis</u> expeditions as we'd like. It was going to take years to complete the project. Then I got an idea."

"For a cheaper instrument?" asked Cousin Lou.

"No. The cost of the instrument doesn't matter so much. It's the speed at which the ship can be operated while it's in use. Time costs money on the <u>Atlantis</u>. With today's instrument the ship must run at six knots. We don't get very far in a day's time."

"What happens with your thing-a-ma-jig?" asked Jeff.

"My thing-a-ma-jig is called a <u>seismic profiler</u>. 'Profiler' for short," laughed Mr. Clark,.

"Tell them what it does," urged Eric.

"It lets scientists gather their data at a ship's speed of thirty knots! We'll be able to cover <u>five</u> <u>times</u> more distance on future trips. Think how that will shorten the project. And the savings will be huge!"

Jeff's and Eric's eyes were gleaming. They were following every word. "So then you had your idea and started working on it in the barn," prompted Jeff. "Go on!"

"Right. That's when I decided to take out insurance. The old barn was paint-parched and tinder dry. Wouldn't even light my pipe out there! Then, when everything was going great guns and my model was nearly finished, the barn burned right to the ground. At night. Roof had caved in before we ever discovered it."

"All those hours of work, gone up in smoke," mourned Miss Kate.

"No need to spell out how you felt. We can guess." Cousin Lou spoke for them all. "What did you do next?"

"Sat around for a whole day with my head in my hands. Then I took a hitch on myself. I'd begin over. But full time, not in bits and snatches!"

"What about your job?" Cousin Lou always thought about the practical angle.

"The Oceanographic gave me a year's leave of absence. I resigned from Town Meeting, from all my commitments. I hired office space in Boston, to be near the big labs and libraries, and did my work there. I had it all figured out. My family would live for a year on the insurance money, while I finished my project."

"Now you're coming to the part nobody understands," broke in Cousin Lou.

"The insurance people came around to investigate the causes of the fire before paying out all that money. Can't say that I blame them. And you wouldn't let them! It caused a lot of talk. Nobody's ever been able to figure out why, Allan."

"I think I know why," Jeff broke in. "Figured it out this afternoon. You were protecting somebody, weren't you?"

There was a dead silence. In the deepening twilight, Jeff could positively feel five pairs of eyes boring into him. "Right you are, boy. That fire was set. I found clear evidence of it. How'd you figure it out?" There was respect in Allan Clark's voice.

Jeff shrugged. "Nothing else made sense. Turning away the investigator cost you a lot of money. There had to be an important reason. I didn't get anywhere until I tried putting myself in your shoes. Guess I'd pass up most anything to protect the folks I care about. Mom and Dad. Even Peg," he grinned.

"So now you've figured out why Dad kept quiet. Let's leave it right there!" Eric jumped to his feet and began to bustle around. "We'd better collect everything and get on home. Mosquitoes are thick as chowder. Anyhow, I've got to roll out about five-thirty tomorrow morning, and Dad's got to drive to Boston...Glad you could come, folks."

Everybody stared at him. "Not a mosquito in sight, young man!" Cousin Lou accused him. "Too much breeze. Stop behaving like a cat on a hot griddle." She settled herself firmly into the sand. "I'm not budging!"

"It's no use, Eric." Allan Clark spoke kindly. "Anybody who knows this much is going to want to know the rest. You would too!"

"At any rate, it's not guesswork any longer, and that's a relief," said Miss Kate. "You youngsters brought in the proof this morning."

Even in the fading light Jeff could feel Cousin Lou's gimlet eyes. "What have you three been up to?" she asked. "It's been mentioned twice tonight."

"We harvested sea moss in Salt Pond, a whole load of it, Miss Bowman. Dredged up a barrel filled with trophies..."

"TROPHIES? In Salt Pond? The trophies that were in your father's barn? But they burned up a year ago!"

"So we thought, Lou," Miss Kate put in. "Turns out otherwise."

"But who'd put them there? And what for?"

"That's what I asked myself!" Jeff said eagerly. "I think I know who put them there. Can't figure out why, though."

Cousin Lou was flabbergasted. "Jeff Cahill, are you telling us you know who fired Allan Clark's barn last year?"

"I really believe he does! Go on and tell us, boy," encouraged Mr. Clark.

"Okay with you, Eric?" Jeff peered into the dusk, trying to make out his friend's face.

"Guess so." Eric's face was gruff. He cleared his throat. "Go ahead. Shoot. Tell 'em, and get it over with. At least they'll know it wasn't Dad!"

"Who said it was? But it was a friend of his, Old Joe. Isn't that right, sir?" Jeff turned toward Mr. Clark.

"Old Joe!" Cousin Lou was flabbergasted. "You're way off course, boy! Old Joe's been devoted to Eric for years. To his dad too, before that."

"He and Mr. Clark had some kind of quarrel, Cousin Lou. Eric told us so."

Allan Clark pulled on his pipe. "The quarrel was my fault," he told them. "The old man was getting more and more feeble and helpless. I did something I don't often do...I stuck my nose in his business. I went to his shack and asked him to let me take him to the Old Folk's Home. There's a good one in town. We could have made regular visits to him."

"What'd he say?" asked Cousin Lou. "Often thought of doing that very thing. Didn't like to interfere, though."

"He was angry. Got as red as a rooster's comb. Said he'd die in a month if he couldn't putter around his own place. I saw he meant it so I picked up my hat and left. It's clear I frightened him. I certainly didn't mean to."

"That still doesn't convince me he set the fire," Cousin Lou insisted stubbornly. "What's your evidence?"

"Whitefoot's my evidence. You know that Old Joe loves Eric. He also loves nature, and all kinds of animals. Eric's horse Whitefoot was let out before the fire started. He had to be! Wasn't a scorched hair on him, and his stall's always padlocked at night!"

Cousin Lou nodded slowly. "Nobody's been able to explain that away. Made it look like a put-up job."

"Remember, Lou, Old Joe didn't know I had an invention in the barn loft. He thought the old rickety building was empty. I think he chose this way to warn me to leave him alone. And I think he's ashamed of what he did. He's been ducking us all ever since. For a while there, we'd find a fat lobster outside our door. But lately he's been too feeble to haul in his pots."

"Shouldn't you have reported him, Allan?" Cousin Lou didn't believe in shirking duty just because it happened to be unpleasant.

"I had no proof," Mr. Clark reminded her. "I was sure in my own mind, but then, lots of folks in town think I set that fire! They've judged me on appearances. I couldn't turn 'round and do the same thing to the old man. Might not have been believed if I'd tried to. Matter of fact, I couldn't even convince Eric. He wouldn't even hear me out!"

"Nobody can say Eric isn't loyal to his friends," declared Miss Kate. "I couldn't make any headway with him either. Nothing could make him believe his old friend set that fire. Then this morning you children turned up the proof."

"It was a weight off my shoulders, let me tell you!" said Allan Clark. "Surmise is one thing. Proof's another."

Cousin Lou was looking mystified, but Eric gave her no time to ask questions. "When I saw the trophies, the jig was up. I knew Dad was right." He heaved a sigh. "Came home and told him so."

Jeff wrinkled his forehead. "That's the part I still don't get, Eric. You'd told us the trophies were kept in the barn. We found them in Salt Pond today. I'm not a moron, so I figured they'd been put there a year ago, before the fire. But why would Old Joe do such a thing? It nearly threw me off the track!"

"Worked just the opposite with me," said Eric. "You see, my name, and my sisters', are engraved on these trophies. When Old Joe went into the barn to set the fire, he saw them there. The names told him they were ours, not Dad's. So he wrapped them carefully in Whitefoot's feed sacks and packed them in a barrel…"

"Got it!" shouted Jeff. "He put them in Salt Pond because he knows you farm it every year! <u>He taught you how</u>! Sooner or later you'd be bound to turn up that barrel. Maybe not until he'd died, though."

"Yep. He wanted us to get them back."

"Seems to me you have a strong case to put before the insurance company, Allan," said Cousin Lou.

"With the trophies in hand, we do," said Mr. Clark. "But I'm sure I speak for both of us when I say that we won't do it as long as the old man lives. Oh, we'll have to report him to the police chief, now that we're sure. The police will keep an eye on him, but I don't think they'll bother him. He hardly leaves his shack these days. Do you agree with me, Kate?"

"Absolutely. If Old Joe felt he wouldn't last a month at the Home, he'd die in a week in jail. We don't want to hasten the old man's death. He's not going to last much longer anyhow. Time enough to put in our claim when he's gone. After the fire we talked it over and decided we could make ends meet somehow, for a year. I took a job at the library. The children have all helped. The girls have done the housework and Eric's tackled the chores. Mountains of odd jobs too, while his father's away. Our troubles have brought us closer together."

"It's been a long and lonely year for all of us," said Mr. Clark. "It's about over, though. I completed my model last week. Gave it a test run two days ago, with a friend who's a geophysicist at Yale." He turned to Jeff and Peg. "Coming back, I happened to board your bus at New Haven."

Cousin Lou got to her feet. "Soon's you release your invention I'll spread the word,' she vowed. "Least I can do." She swallowed hard. "Allan," she said, "Reckon there's no way 'round it. I ask your pardon!" She stretched out her hand.

Mr. Clark grasped it firmly. "Now that didn't come easy to you, Lou. It's freely granted."

"These children deserve the credit," said Cousin Lou. "They did a lot more than turn up the trophies and give you your proof. They opened my eyes in ways you'll never hear about." She turned to Eric. "Come over tomorrow, boy, and sample a very special pie. I owe you one! There's no fool like an old fool!"

"We share the blame too, Lou. It's wasn't all your fault," said Miss Kate. "You wouldn't ask, but we wouldn't explain."

"Maybe it's because you're all Cape Codders," said Jeff, and everybody laughed.

"Time to forget the whole thing and have some fun," declared Mr. Clark. "I'm giving myself a full ten days off before reporting back to work."

"He's earned a holiday," approved Miss Kate.

Allan Clark ruffled Eric's hair. "Want to hear my holiday plans? I'll teach you kids to sail, starting tomorrow morning. We'll go to the big dunes at Truro, too. We'll ride beach buggies all the way from there to the lighthouse at Provincetown..."

"Suits me," said Eric. "Saw some fellows doing that in a newsreel."

"Next, I'll give you a conducted tour of the Oceanographic Institution. ALVIN, the Navy's baby submarine, is tied up at the dock there this week."

"You mean the one that helped find the hydrogen bomb in the ocean off Spain?" asked Jeff. "I read a book about that."

"That's the one. We'll go aboard the <u>Atlantis</u>, too."

"Hurrah!" shouted Jeff. "Will they let us?" He added anxiously.

"No trouble about that." Mr. Clark smiled. "My stock's pretty high with the crew of the <u>Atlantis</u>!" He turned to Eric. "You like to farm Salt Pond, son. Some day you may farm the <u>floor</u> <u>of</u> <u>the</u> <u>ocean</u>! There'll be lots more people in the world, and that requires more food to feed them. Then, we really ought to take a boat excursion to Nantucket..."

"And to Martha's Vineyard," interrupted Eric. "Wait till they see those rainbow-colored cliffs at Gay Head. Real Indians live there!"

His father nodded. "We'll to deep sea fishing one day. For stripers and for bluefish. Jeff and Peg would like that." He turned to Peg. "How does all this strike you, young lady?"

For once, Peg had nothing to say. Only her glowing eyes spoke for her.

"Seems to me you'll be right busy," laughed Miss Kate. "Sounds like a full schedule to me!"

"Oh boy, it sounds like <u>heaven</u> to me! Jeff turned gratefully to Cousin Lou. "Gosh, how can we ever thank you for inviting us?" he asked. "Peg and I think you're just the greatest! We'll never forget our visit, Cousin Lou. All this fun, and we're learning so many new things, too!"

For a minute Cousin Lou didn't say a word. "I'm not apt to forget your visit either," she said dryly. Then her eyes twinkled, and the corners of her mouth turned up. "Fact of the matter is, I've learned a thing or two myself!"

ABOUT THE AUTHOR

A.B. degree Radcliffe College. Was Editor-in-Chief *Child Life* magazine for 13 years. Published many articles in national magazines, (*Town and Country*, *Harper's Bazaar*,etc. had one article reprinted in *Readers Digest*). Published a juvenile novel *Adventure on the Cloud 9* with G.P. Putnam &

Sons, and two books with Houghton-Mifflin (one juvenile biography, one adult non-fiction). Was a columnist for *The National Observer* for 3 years. The column, entitled *Zoo's Who*, won their prestigious Laurel Award for most popular column. Has had many poems published, two in major anthologies, and an earlier book of poetry.

Has won 3 national senior Olympic gold medals and one silver, and one USTA senior national title, in tennis. Has lectured on juvenile writing at Radcliffe Course in Publishing Procedures and at the Boston Center of Adult Education. She lives of Cape Cod.

CPSIA information can be obtained at www.ICGtesting.com
Printed in the USA
LVOW11s1108020315

428902LV00001B/21/P